Victoria had been Benedict Gabriell's secretary for eight years, so she knew him pretty well—and an impossible, dictatorial man he was too! So would marrying him, knowing all his faults already, be the most sensible thing she could do—or was she heading for disaster?

THIS SIDE
OF HEAVEN

BY

ALEXANDRA SCOTT

MILLS & BOON LIMITED
15–16 BROOK'S MEWS
LONDON W1A 1DR

First published 1982
Australian copyright 1982
Philippine copyright 1982
This edition 1982

© Alexandra Scott 1982

ISBN 0 263 73998 8

Set in Monophoto Times 11 on 11½ pt.
05–1082 – 50751

Made and printed in Great Britain by
Richard Clay (The Chaucer Press) Ltd,
Bungay, Suffolk

CHAPTER ONE

'Of course the answer is no. It's quite impossible.'
Victoria forced the words from stiff lips while she
gazed at the man whom she had known for eight
years. At least, she had worked for him for eight
years, but there were some aspects of his life about
which she knew as little as she had on that first
day, when she had presented herself at his office, a
nervous eighteen-year-old, fresh from secretarial
college. There they had been told that no man is a
hero to his secretary, and so it had been with
Benedict Gabriell, who could be utterly ruthless in
his demands, totally inconsiderate in his treatment,
and then when she had decided that the breaking
point had been reached, with one of those sudden
changes of mood, he would exert himself to be
charming.

No, certainly Victoria had no illusions about the
man. He could in the course of a morning be ex-
asperating, impatient, irritable, demonic often, so
that if he had had a wife it would have been hard
indeed not to pity her. In fact she had often reflected with her employer very much in mind that
what was true of secretaries was very likely true of
wives as well. And now he was suggesting . . .

He got up from his desk and sauntered towards
her with that easy careless graceful stride which
she knew so well. Even his gait told her what kind
of mood he was in. Today he was setting himself

5

out quite deliberately to disarm, to beguile and to charm. She knew the symptoms only too well and although she wasn't often at the receiving end, she knew too how effective such an approach invariably was.

'Think about it, Miss Kendall. You might find the idea growing on you.' He smiled, showing the dazzling teeth, just like a toothpaste ad, she had told herself once in a mood of exasperation as she watched him use his powerful charm with considerable effect. But even as the idea had run through her mind she had known that there was much more to him than that. Handsome and attractive he might be, but there were other qualities, profound depths which she had not yet fathomed.

The tawny-gold eyes glinted as if he could read her thoughts and was amused by them. 'And then,' he continued after what seemed to Victoria a long time, 'I'm sure you would come to realise that marriage would have decided advantages for both of us, Miss Kendall.'

The light amused laugh, wholly false, issuing from Victoria's lips cost her an effort, but she was glad she had made it. 'Don't you find it slightly ridiculous, Mr Gabriell, that you're proposing to me, yet you still think of me as Miss Kendall?' She got up from her chair in front of and slightly to the left of his desk where she had been sitting with pencil poised ready to take notes for next month's television programme. The nervous shock of his proposal made her step behind the chair as if for protection. 'The perfect secretary, I suppose.' Her brown eyes gave an impression of amusement as she struggled to return his look calmly.

'I shall call you Victoria soon enough if you give me the answer I want. As you say, you're the perfect secretary,' he shrugged, the wide shoulders under the silk shirt rippling the thin material. 'Or at least as perfect as I'm likely to find this side of heaven. And I've a feeling that you might turn out to be the perfect wife as well for a man in my position.'

'Now we're coming to it.' All at once Victoria felt herself seething with anger which she fought to control. 'A man in your position! Whatever that means.' She waited and when he did not answer but continued to gaze at her although with faintly narrowed eyes she continued, 'Why should you propose to me when every gossip column in Fleet Street is expecting to hear of your engagement to the Baroness Kertesz?'

If Victoria had been less emotional she would have noticed the way his lips tightened and would have heeded the warning. When he spoke his voice was dangerously quiet. 'Surely you know me well enough to understand that I'm not responsible for the wild imaginings of every hack journalist who has nothing better to do?'

'It's a pity,' Victoria drew a shuddering breath as she took the opportunity to say something she would never have dared to hint at in the ordinary way, 'it's a great pity that over the years you've given them so much ammunition. Since I've worked for you I don't think you've been out of the news for more than a fortnight at a time.'

'Tut, tut, Miss Kendall! I didn't know that you were interested in such trashy papers.' The lightness of his manner was belied by the thin tight gash of his lips. 'I'm sorry your prim scruples have been offended.' Their eyes clashed and held, until at last Victoria looked away. There was a long silence during which the girl sought feverishly for something to say, something which might give her the opportunity to retreat in the direction of her own office where she could give way to her overwrought feelings. But her mind remained stubbornly, treacherously blank and it was her employer who had the satisfaction of continuing.

'But maybe you've found the answer to your own question, Miss Kendall. Maybe I'm getting just a little bit tired of being the focus for so many third-rate writers in Fleet Street.' His eyes narrowed as his intense gaze raked her mercilessly. 'Maybe I think I've reached an age when I ought to settle down.' His smile was suddenly mischievous, totally bewildering to the girl who was trying to retain some slight grip on reality. 'But I shan't avoid the issue any longer. It was a reasonable question and deserves some explanation. I've nothing against marriage, Miss Kendall. In fact some people,' he underlined those two words, 'would be surprised to know just how conventional I am in that respect. But where I differ from most men, and most women too, I dare say, is that I've always thought the arranged marriage had everything to recommend it.'

'Arranged marriage!' At last Victoria found her tongue and was able to inject a certain amount of scorn into her repetition of his words. 'How ridiculously old-fashioned!'

'As you say.' Aggravatingly he showed no sign of annoyance at her scoffing. 'But as marriage is likely to be the most important decision in anyone's life then I think it should be made intelligently. After all, one wouldn't buy a house solely on appearance or situation. You would want to know all about it, have a surveyor's report. You would do the same for any business deal, read the small print in any contract, not depend on anything as fickle as one's emotions.'

'But it isn't a business deal. It's so much more than that.'

'That's why it's so important. And I know you're tailor-made for me.'

'I don't see why if it's vital for you to get a woman made to fit your own special requirements you don't just go to a marriage bureau. I'm sure,' she battled with the bitterness in her voice, 'they'd be queuing up for the job.'

'But why go to that trouble,' now he was laughing at her, 'when I have the prototype right here on the premises? Can you imagine the fatigue of it, Miss Kendall? Entertaining this queue of young women, judging them all against you. Finding them wanting, then having to come back to you and throw myself on your mercy.' As his eyes travelled slowly over her disturbed features the spark of amusement faded from his eyes.

'Think about it, Miss Kendall, that's all I'm asking.' The unexpected gentleness in his voice made her want to weep. 'Don't answer now. Think about it as you would any other business proposition, because that's exactly what I'm putting to you.' Negligently he leaned against the desk beside her, all trace of his former irritation concealed if not forgotten. Then he smiled, that emotion-jolting expression she had seen used with such devastating effect on so many occasions. 'I suppose I've been wrong to spring this on you suddenly. I ought to have been more devious, have laid on soft lights and sweet music. But I paid you the compliment of thinking that you would despise such evasiveness and that a straightforward proposal of marriage would . . .'

'I wouldn't marry you,' the words burst from Victoria's mouth before she could stop them, 'if you . . .'

'Please don't say "if I were the last man in the world".' The laughter, real or assumed in his voice mocked her. 'I expect something much more original from you, Miss Kendall, not the words you might hear in a "B" film of the forties.'

'I wouldn't know,' Victoria said nastily, 'I wasn't around then.'

Opposite her she saw the straight dark eyebrows raised, a considering expresion on his face. 'No,' he sounded as if he weren't absolutely certain, 'no, I suppose you wouldn't be.' He heaved himself away from the desk and took a step towards her. 'And it might surprise you to know that I wasn't either—at least not as a student of second rate features in the cinema. But come on now, Miss Kendall,' abruptly he went round to the far side of his desk and sat down, 'let's stop hurling insults at each other. In a game like that you're bound to be the loser. I want you to take some notes about next month's programme . . .' He frowned with the concentration he brought to all his work and Victoria slid into her seat, totally bemused and wondering if she had imagined that strange inter-

lude. If so, she thought as she feverishly typed out
the pages of notes he had subsequently dictated, it
was time she saw a doctor!

She was still confused as she drove home that
night through the busy rush-hour traffic of central
London, stopping and starting at traffic lights with
all the interest of a sleepwalker until with a tiny
sigh of relief she turned into the courtyard of the
smart block of flats where she had lived for the
past three years. That was one advantage of working for a man like Benedict Gabriell. He was
absurdly generous and carried you along on the
tide of his affluence and could afford things
hitherto beyond reach and expectation.

Victoria closed the door of her flat, leaning
against it for a moment before walking very slowly
to the bathroom. When she had had a shower she
felt better, but before she went into the kitchen to
begin making a meal she sat down at her dressing-
table to study herself in the mirror.

Certainly she was as unlike Benedict Gabriell's
usual girl-friends as it was possible to be. While
they were either raven black or dazzling blonde,
she was simply mouse. Someone had once de-
scribed her hair as molten gold, but since then it
had darkened somewhat, and in any case he had
been suffering from too much champagne at the
wedding they had just left. Her eyes she had always
considered her best feature, for they were large,
slanted very slightly, brown with long sooty lashes.
Apart from that her face had little to recommend
it, for while her nose was straight, the mouth was a
bit large.

Her figure was good enough, although even there

she didn't match up to the willowy shape her boss
seemed to prefer. Victoria held her thin housecoat
against her still damp body. She did have a bust,
her waist was small in proportion, but her hips . . .
She wasn't sure at all. Just that she wasn't what he
had seemed to be interested in.

In fact in all the years she had been working for
him, Benedict Gabriell had never shown by the
slightest hint, by the most faintly admiring glance,
that he had noticed her sex was the opposite one
from his own.

Victoria shivered and got up from the dressing
stool. It was going to be awkward for a few days,
until the aberration was forgotten. It was fortunate
that he had had an appointment with his pro-
ducer this afternoon, as he had left the office while
she was at lunch and she had been able to leave
without seeing him.

The telephone shrilled wildly startling her from
her reverie.

'Hello.' She couldn't think who her caller might
be, she was expecting no one. Her girl friend had
just left to take up an appointment in Brussels and
the submariner whom she had been dating recently
was somewhere beneath the waves of the Baltic.

'Miss Kendall.' The familiar voice made her
shake. 'I shall be round to take you out to dinner.
About eight o'clock.'

Before she could catch her breath to reply the
line went dead. Before she could tell him that she
wouldn't go out with him if he were the last man
on earth. It would have been so much easier on the
phone than telling him to his face when he came
round to collect her.

'Will you look this way, Mrs Gabriell.'

'Put your arm round her, Ben. Just one last shot—that's it!'

'When did you two decide to get married?'

'Wasn't it rather sudden?'

'Are you going to continue to work as Mr Gabriell's secretary now that you're married to him, Mrs Gabriell?'

'Did you know that Baroness Kertesz is returning to London shortly, Mr Gabriell?'

'Over here, Mrs Gabriell. Smile for just a moment—fine. Thanks!'

'What would you say the colour of that dress is, Mrs Gabriell?'

Victoria stood with a fixed smile on her face, startled by all the flashes from camera lights, stunned by the noise and the questions and trying to be unaware of Benedict's arm circling her waist. She sensed that his voice was calm and unruffled, even faintly amused by the impudent prying of the reporters.

'We decided some time ago,' he lied blatantly.

'No, it wasn't sudden. But I had to use my powers of persuasion.' In the ripple of laughter Victoria recognised incredulity. What girl, it seemed to ask, would play hard to get with Benedict Gabriell? Especially a girl like the one he had just married.

'Are you going to go on working for Mr Gabriell now that you're married?' the little girl reporter wearing jeans and a yellow tee-shirt persisted.

'Go on, answer them, darling.' Benedict's face smiled down at her.

'I'm not sure.' Her voice was low and slightly breathless. 'I don't think he's found a replacement yet.'

'No,' her husband replied to the persistent question about the baroness, 'we don't keep each other informed about our every move.'

'As far as I know she hasn't heard about our marriage. Even our parents don't know. Yes,' without looking Victoria knew that he was frowning, sensed that his patience was running out, 'yes, when she does know I'm certain she'll be pleased.'

'So last week's story in Julia's Diary in the *Sketch* was wrong, Mr Gabriell?' the tall laconic reporter persevered. 'About you and the Baroness getting engaged?'

'It looks like it, Tom.' Obviously Benedict knew the man. 'They've been wrong before, as I think you'll be aware. And if they were right I would scarcely be here now, would I?' His arm round Victoria's waist tightened, pulling her against him. 'And now, if you'll excuse us, I really want to get my wife to myself.'

There was a faint clapping while flashbulbs continued to pop and the two television cameras rolled feverishly. Benedict began to push his way through the throng pressing round them, determined to reach the long sleek car parked at the kerb.

'Can you tell me the colour of your dress, Mrs Gabriell?' The girl reporter waited with pencil poised, the blue eyes looking not at Victoria but, rather dazedly, at the tall bridegroom, handsome and distinguished in a dark suit.

'Oh, in the shop they said it was avocado mousse.' Victoria smoothed down the filmy pleats as they swirled around her slender legs.

'And you don't feel superstitious about wearing green for your wedding?' Reluctantly the girl dragged her eyes away from the bridegroom, but without appearing to listen to Victoria's reply.

'Where are you going for the honeymoon?'

At last they reached the car and Benedict was handing her into the passenger seat. She watched him thrust his way round the bonnet of the car, saw him grin at something one of the television men said to him, and felt herself blush as she imagined what the casual comment might have been.

Then he slid into the driving seat and they were nosing their way through the crowd, along the narrow street until the main thoroughfare was reached and soon they were skimming amid all the early afternoon traffic along Park Lane in the direction of Benedict's flat. There was silence in the car, a hint of tension that made Victoria dart a glance at the man who sat so tight-lipped and grim at the wheel of the car.

'I can't imagine how the press got hold of the story.' She stared straight ahead, scarcely aware that the sun was shining, that they were moving through a chequered world of light and shade. 'You were so insistent that no one should be told.'

'Oh . . .' she sensed that one of his black moods was on him, '. . . I can explain that. I rang Phil Westmacott this morning and told him.'

'You . . . you what?' For a moment Victoria was convinced that she had misheard him speak the name of the *Clarion*'s editor.

'I thought as they were bound to hear in any event.'

'But . . .' her voice was as cold as she felt herself, 'but you were so insistent that I shouldn't mention it to anyone.'

'Well, you can't expect to keep these things secret for long.'

'I don't suppose it occurs to you that perhaps I would have preferred to let my own parents know first. It was only because of your attitude that I kept silent. Now,' to her dismay she heard her voice tremble just a little, 'now they're bound to hear it from television this evening. At least,' she couldn't resist the little waspish dig, 'if it's considered important enough to make the news.'

'I don't think there's any doubt about that.' It was said so matter-of-factly that she couldn't even accuse him of conceit. 'At least,' he darted a quick grin at her which she only half saw, 'short of a world war having begun in the meantime. And as far as your family is concerned then you can ring whenever you get in. My mother doesn't know yet either, of course.' He spoke with such confidence that she concluded he didn't even think the matter required an apology, and Victoria wondered rebelliously what his reaction would have been had the situation been reversed and she had been the one to inform the world about their sudden marriage.

But before she could say any more the car turned right, out of the main flow of traffic, across the secluded square, stopping in a quiet cul-de-sac of elegant town houses. Victoria turned to face the man she had just married, uncomfortably aware of something like panic mounting inside her.

'Now for the first hurdle.' She saw Benedict's lips moving, heard his voice as if it was coming from a long way. 'I've got to break it to Lumsden that I've got myself a wife.'

'Lumsden?' She had no idea who he was talking about.

'My man.' He smiled at her encouragingly, then getting out came round and helped her out. 'Lumsden has been looking after me for the past ten months, ever since the Jacksons retired.'

'Oh.' As she crossed the pavement to the royal purple front door, Victoria thought again how little she knew of him. There had always been a secrecy about him which had insisted that the two parts of his life were kept separate, and she knew nothing of what went on behind this solid-looking door with the polished worn lion's mask which was even now being rattled loudly.

She had no idea whether to be relieved or disappointed that Benedict ignored the tradition of carrying the bride over the threshold. When she thought of it later she was rather pleased that she had not been required to undergo the ordeal under Lumsden's disapproving eye.

For it was clear enough that the surprise news did not make pleasant hearing for the man who opened the door to Benedict's imperious summons. Of course he said all the expected things, but the moment Victoria looked into the cold blue eyes she knew she was not a welcome addition at 12 Peverell Square.

'Married? Indeed, sir? Let me congratulate you. And you too, madam. But this is a surprise. If I had known, sir, I could have prepared some kind of celebration . . .'

'Oh, that doesn't matter. We'll have some tea later, Lumsden, and I shall be taking Mrs Gabriell out to dinner, so there's no need to worry.'

'I see, sir. But . . .' he hesitated, 'am I to understand, sir, that you and . . .' he smiled at Victoria, 'the new Mrs Gabriell are going to be staying here tonight? You're not going off,' he coughed delicately, '. . . on holiday?'

Victoria turned away to study one of a series of small prints hanging on the white walls of the hallway, hoping that no one would notice the flaming colour of her checks. She heard her husband answer without the least sign of embarrassment. 'No, we're not going away just yet. Later perhaps when all my commitments have been dealt with. Oh, and Lumsden, I'll just take Mrs Gabriell into the sitting room, then I'd like to see you about preparing a bedroom.'

'Yes, sir. Of course, sir.' Lumsden turned to go in the direction of the kitchen. 'And once again sir, madam . . .' he bowed slightly, 'my heartiest congratulations to you both.'

The room into which Benedict led Victoria was so attractive that for a moment she almost forgot her feelings of apprehension and unhappiness.

'Oh, Benedict . . .' She walked forward to the huge windows that opened out on to the garden. 'How lovely it is!' She turned to smile at the tall dark figure lounging watchfully against the closed door. 'I'm always surprised that these town houses have such lovely gardens.' She coloured slightly as he levered himself upright and came towards her, looking like a total stranger in the formal suit with the red rose in his buttonhole. As of course he was.

'Do you realise that is the first time you've used my name as if I were slightly more to you than an employer?'

She gazed at him, trying to discern whether or not he was amused, but on the whole decided he was not. 'Less than a week ago, that's just what you were.' She spoke softly, with an air of shyness which made her lips tremble. 'It's all so strange— for you as much as for me.'

He smiled as he came closer to her, then put out one hand to circle her neck in a gesture that was tender but without passion. 'Of course it is. But it'll be all right, you'll see.' The curious yellowy eyes travelled over her slowly, from the single black silk rose in a spray of veiling on her hair to her feet in high-heeled patent black shoes. 'And I would be a pretty unsatisfactory sort of husband if I didn't tell you how pretty you look.' His hand moved to touch the collar of her dress. 'And I'm glad you chose green, it's my favourite colour. Now,' he dropped his hand as if afraid he had said too much, 'now I must make arrangements with Lumsden about your room . . .' He turned from her to the door only looking round at her exclamation.

'But . . .'

'Yes?' He raised an enquiring eyebrow.

'Won't Lumsden think it strange . . .?'

For a moment he stared blankly, then his face cleared. 'Oh, you mean he'll be surprised that we aren't sharing a bedroom?' He seemed to find no embarrassment in the words that she had been so reluctant to speak, merely shrugging briefly. 'That doesn't matter. Lumsden isn't paid to think about

our private affairs. Besides, he's been in service
long enough to know that people have some very
curious private arrangements. In any case, I've
decided we'll have adjoining rooms.' The raised
eyebrow challenged her to object and when she did
not reply he went on, 'With a connecting door, if
you have no objections. We each have a bathroom,
so you can feel perfectly secure. You can even lock
the door if you think that's necessary.' Victoria felt
a stab of pain at such barbed advice, but her impassive expression showed nothing of her feelings.
'Oh, and,' Benedict turned, his hand reaching out
for the doorknob, 'just sit down and I'll get
Lumsden to bring tea in a moment.'

Victoria did as she was told. Or rather she
subsided on to the large dark green velvet settee
because her legs refused to support her any longer.
Without seeing them she stared at the fireplace with
the polished steel canopy and gleaming fire-irons,
her eyes moving restlessly over the modern sculp-
tures in the alcoves at each side.

What had she done? The madness which had
possessed her for ten days slipped from her with
shattering suddenness. What foolish impulse had
led her to this impossible situation with this man?
If only she could turn the clock back to that day
when he had made his startling suggestion, to the
evening of the day when he had ordered her to
have dinner with him. She ought never to have
gone. She should have ignored the persistent ringing of the doorbell when he came to collect her.

Instead she had done what every other woman
would have done. She had pandered to his male
vanity, had rushed to her wardrobe, had dragged

out that new dress she had been saving for a special occasion and had pulled it over her head with trembling fingers. She had gone with him and had allowed herself to fall under the influence of his charm. Just as she had watched, cynically, a hundred others softening, being moulded under his spell. Even when he had repeated his proposal, matter-of-factly, demonstrating his belief that their outing was a business dinner just like any other, she could hardly believe it was her own voice murmuring the acceptance.

And when she had seen the smile of pleasure and just a little smug satisfaction, but no surprise, on his face it gave her the strength to decide on the pose she must adopt.

'I'm delighted you've changed your mind.' He raised his glass smiling at her over the rim. 'Might I ask why?'

'Of course.' Victoria shrugged with all the composure she could effect while praying he wouldn't notice the trembling of her glass as she responded to his silent toast. 'I suppose you could say that you've trained me well,' she gave a little self-deprecating smile. 'You put a proposition to *me*, the business woman you've created in your image.' Her manner was as hardboiled as she could make it. 'I suppose that in the circumstances it would have been stranger still if I *hadn't* accepted. You were right.' Her eyes smiled brilliantly at him. 'When I had had time to think it over of course I couldn't refuse. Now, I can see that it's a perfect business arrangement, one I'd have to be a fool to pass up.'

When they had returned to her flat he had stood

for just a moment in the hallway. 'I'm glad, Victoria. I know it'll be a great success—you're that sort of girl.' Then he had gone, closing the door quietly behind him. He hadn't even bothered to kiss her and she tried to assure herself that she was glad. After all, she thought with a wry twist of her lips, he didn't usually sign his contracts with a kiss and she was glad to be spared the hypocrisy. At least he hadn't pretended he was madly in love. She had gone to bed, had slept soundly in spite of the occasion.

Next morning she should have run from him. She should have got into her car and she ought not to have stopped driving until she reached Yorkshire. And she should have told her mother to telephone her employer the news that she was suffering from a mental breakdown and would be unable to return to work for at least six months.

Even earlier she should have run from him. That first morning when she had appeared in his office, when he had raised an exasperated face towards her from the disorganised pile of papers on his desk.

'Well?' He frowned.

'I . . . knocked. No one seemed to hear, so I came in.'

'You came in.' He picked up a half-smoked cigarette from an overflowing ashtray. 'Straight from the frozen north, I presume.'

'The frozen north?' She stared, nervous, uncomprehending.

'A joke, a joke,' he said wearily. Then with exaggerated politeness, 'Do I detect a trace of Yorkshire in your speech?'

'Yes.' Awkwardly she had coloured. 'I'm . . . I'm sorry.'

'Don't be, my dear child.' She wasn't certain whether he was laughing at her or not. 'It's the merest trace and not unattractive. But what can I do for you? If it's the crammers you want that's downstairs.'

'The crammers?' she had queried.

'There's a school downstairs where they try to force the unwilling through their O-levels. Down one.' With the air of having devoted more time to her than he could afford, he returned to the papers on his desk with an air of desperate concentration.

'No, I . . . I think it's you I want. That is if you're Mr Gabriell.' It pleased her to pretend that he wasn't instantly recognisable.

'Me?' He raised his head to look at her and for a moment his expression was so bewildered that Victoria had to repress an overwhelming inclination to giggle. Then he had closed his eyes, covered his face with one hand and groaned aloud. 'No, don't tell me. Please, not again. The agency.' He opened his eyes again and looked, no, he glared at her. 'The Excelsior Secretarial Agency.' Again he made a sound, this time half-way between a laugh and a groan. 'Excelsior, they call themselves!'

While she listened to him, Victoria could feel herself shrinking, but she realised that this was one battle she must not allow to slip away. Inexperienced as she was she understood that this man was one who would wipe his feet on you if he could get away with it, the kind they had been warned about at college, the original of the If Your

Boss Is A Beast talk given by one of the visiting tutors.

'Yes, I'm from the agency.' She tried to talk crisply, as she imagined perfect secretaries did, at the same time opening her bag and taking out a pad and pencil. 'Of course I quite understand that you'll want to test me out before you engage me.'

'Engage you?' His drawl defeated all her attempts at self-possession and she felt a blush start in the soles of her feet and work its way up. Meanwhile she stared as if mesmerised by the peculiar yellow-gold eyes. 'That's out of the question, I'm afraid.' He watched with sadistic amusement as the colour in her cheeks deepened. 'You see,' he appeared to take a little pity on her for he turned away, 'I specifically asked for a mature woman, not someone who's just left the school-room and who'll spend half of her time on the tele-phone to boy-friends. Then just when we're getting used to each other she'll get married and have a baby at the most inconvenient time possible.' He pulled the typewriter across the desk, frowning irritably as he fed a sheet of paper into the roller.

'I don't have any boy-friends in London.' It seemed unnecessary to inform him that she had no girl friends either. 'So I'm unlikely to spend all my time on the telephone. Or,' she allowed herself a glimmer of humour, 'have a baby when it's in-convenient for you.'

'Hmm.' He paused to use a rubber on the work he had just typed and looked at her briefly, with little interest. 'Perhaps not. But it won't be long. I know what you girls are like when the glamour of the big city hits you. After all the repressions of the frozen north . . .'

'Harrogate isn't exactly the North Pole. And they do have good secretarial colleges there.'

'A girl from secretarial college isn't exactly what I had in mind. Invariably they know nothing and most of them can't even spell.'

'Very well,' Victoria tried to hide her seething anger under a calmly frigid exterior, 'I can see that you would be impossible to work for, and I'm not surprised that your last secretary has gone.' Without hurrying she replaced her notebook and pencil and turned to the door. She was running down the stairs when a shout from above her head made her pause and look up.

'Hey, you! Miss . . . er . . .'

'Do you mean me?' She glared at him, hoping the distance between them would not diminish the effect of her displeasure.

'Yes, of course you. I can't see anyone else on the stairs, can you? Can you do filing, answering the telephone, making coffee, that sort of thing?'

'Ye—es,' she stammered slowly. 'But that's not what I'm trained to do.'

'Oh, come back up here.' The dark head hanging over the banisters disappeared and she heard the door of his office bang closed.

Reluctantly but with a feeling of excitement she couldn't quite ignore, she climbed up to the landing, straightened the belt of her new dress and went inside. 'Yes?' From the doorway she stood looking at him.

'You can start on these.' He pushed a bulging tray of letters towards her. 'I'm sure you'll be able to pick up Janet's filing system as you go along.'

'Do you . . . do you . . . mean you want to engage me?'

'Well, so long as you understand that it's only a temporary job. Janet has taken three months' leave and then she's coming back. But if you care to help out until then I'm sure I'll be able to manage. Anything important I'll send out to a typing agency. You might be able to cope with the run-of-the-mill stuff.'

'Thank you.' But her sarcasm was lost on him and she wasn't inclined to underline it in case he should change his mind. The most important thing for her at the moment was to find a job. She hadn't realised quite how expensive living in London would be, and she would do anything rather than go back home to the job in her father's office.

'Oh, and by the way, Miss . . . whatever your name is, I'm not impossible to work for. As I said, Janet left because she was expecting a baby and,' he grinned suddenly, disarmingly, 'I don't want to have an experience like that again in a hurry! Rushing through the traffic at one in the afternoon simply because she'd got her dates wrong!'

Victoria blushed again, but tried to disguise it by scooping up the contents of the letter tray and turning towards the filing cabinets which lined one wall. 'Oh, and my name's Kendall,' she told him. 'Victoria Kendall.'

'Right, Miss Kendall.' He sounded abstracted as he stabbed at the typewriter keys with two fingers. 'Oh, and in case you have any ideas about it, I have no influence with television producers and can't do anything if you have ideas in that direction.'

'Television?' She turned to look at him, all wide-eyed innocence. 'I'm sorry, I don't understand, Mr Gabriell.'

'No?' He looked at her through half-closed suspicious eyes. 'Well, in that case it doesn't matter.'

And at that moment Victoria was glad to think that she had had the last word. How was he to know that in the frozen north of Harrogate his television programmes were as popular as ever they were in Chelsea? Market research excepted, of course.

But by the end of the first week she was madly in love. Just like ninety per cent of the other women he wiped his feet on. Only in Victoria's case it was a despairing emotion, something she fought resolutely and resisted with all her might. And even at the end of eight years she was very confident that not by one single inflection of her voice, not by a softening of her eyes, had she ever betrayed herself to him.

How she would have hated him to know, to have the pleasure of adding another scalp to his belt. And if ever she had shown her feelings by the slightest hint, she would have had no choice but to leave. For Janet, when she had returned to the office to let them know that after all she couldn't bear the thought of leaving her baby son, had told her about an earlier secretary.

'Well, you know what he's like.' Janet had sat on the edge of Victoria's desk and jerked her head towards the inner sanctum. 'He just has to look at a girl with those tiger's eyes. That's what happened with the girl before me, she began to get all moony about him, all heavy breathing over the paper clips.

That's why he insisted on someone married when I applied.'

'Mmm.' London's sophistication was beginning to rub off on Victoria. 'From what I've seen, he shouldn't be averse to that—the female adoration, I mean.'

'No, he's not. But not in the office. That's why he's inclined to keep you at arm's length. You might have noticed. But,' she smiled comfortingly, 'he'll be all right with you.'

And for eight years she had been with him, sometimes seething with anger at his lack of consideration, often disagreeing violently with an opinion he expressed in one of his television shows, frequently loathing him with all the hatred of which she was capable.

But all the time loving him, tenderly, passionately and altogether hopelessly.

And love, thought Victoria with a feeling of absolute despair, was no sort of basis for a marriage like theirs.

CHAPTER TWO

'You don't have to watch your weight, do you . . . Victoria?' That minute pause before he spoke her name told her that he had almost said Miss Kendall. The thought brought an instant pain to her chest which she knew wanted relief in a bout of weeping.

'No, I don't. It's just that Lumsden has gone overboard a bit with his afternoon tea. It's a far cry from the cup of tea and digestive biscuit that we usually have in the office.'

'I know what you mean.' Benedict surveyed the heavily laden trolley with a slightly jaundiced eye and rose from the easy chair at the side of the fireplace. 'We'll just be in time to catch the news.' He gave the impression of being anxious for any diversion.

Without really thinking about it, Victoria sat looking at the day's reports on the early evening bulletin. It was hard to imagine that they had been married less than four hours. They were sitting here talking like strangers thrown together briefly in a railway carriage and he hadn't troubled to hide his restlessness. She would hardly have been surprised if he had suggested going back to the office to catch up with some work.

On the numerous occasions when she had tried unsuccessfully to ring her parents, Benedict had sat watching broodily as if resenting the disturbance

29

her presence was causing in his well-ordered life. And when just about ten minutes ago she had put down the receiver with a gesture of impatience, he had sighed so that she got the message of his exasperation.

Suddenly, aware that she was hearing something familiar, her gaze concentrated on the picture in front of them. On the screen there she was, surrounded by shouting reporters, Benedict deflecting their questions with expert assurance. She glanced at him, surprising a cynical twist on his lips which he didn't trouble to hide. The announcer's words drew her attention again.

'. . . a complete surprise to their friends. The new Mrs Gabriell has been her husband's secretary for some time and it is understood that she will be continuing to assist both in his television work and in the field of travel writing for which Mr Gabriell is also well known.'

Victoria glanced again at her husband, wondering how he would take this interpretation of her role. She could imagine that he might consider this too inflating for someone who had never been more than a mere secretary. But before she could deduce anything from his expression the telephone rang shrilly, imperatively at his elbow.

'Hello.' He frowned against the background of the noise from the television so that Victoria rose to turn down the sound. 'Oh, hello, darling.' She paused, her fingers frozen to the knob, her heart hammering against her chest. She stood there, staring away from him, surprised that such a perfect summer evening should be so sad, so oppressive. She listened to the deep chuckle. 'Yes,

Mother, I know we've been secretive.' Victoria released her breath in a little shuddering gasp and rubbed her hands down her arms as if she were cold. She walked towards the door and heard Benedict saying, 'Yes, she's here now. Yes, of course. Yes, that's right—her mother doesn't know either. Victoria!' He stopped her just as she was about to go out of the door. 'My mother would like to speak to you.' He put a hand over the mouthpiece. 'Smooth her down if you can . . .' Then into the receiver, 'Here she is, darling. And I hope you'll be more charming to her than you have been to me.' He laughed again as he handed the instrument to his wife.

'Hello.' She was conscious of his eyes watching her closely. 'Yes. Yes. I'm sorry you had to hear from the television. It was wrong of us, I know.'

'Oh well,' the soft voice at the other end laughed reluctantly, 'I suppose I shall have to forgive you—especially as I'm rather pleased about it. I'd given up the idea of a daughter-in-law and grandchildren. Now tell me, my dear, when are you coming down to see me?'

'I . . . I don't know.' Helplessly Victoria looked at Benedict and held the receiver slightly away from her head so that he could hear too.

'What about next weekend?' Benedict nodded rather grimly. 'From what I heard on the local news . . .' Mrs Gabriell laughed, 'Oh yes, it's been on that too, with slightly more detail than on the national news. They said that the honeymoon's being delayed until Ben has finished this series of television interviews next month. But a long week-end in Cornwall should be quite pleasant. After all, honeymooners have been coming here for years.'

Victoria was glad that Benedict had moved away and was unlikely to have heard what his mother was saying. 'Yes, I think that will be all right. Shall we leave it until we've made the arrangements and let you know about the time we expect to come?' After a few more trivialities she put down the receiver and glanced at the man who was lying back in the chair looking at her with such a closed peculiar expression. It was a long time before he spoke.

'Well, that's someone who sounds pleased.'

'I'm glad there's someone.'

Without looking at him she knew that the sharpness of her tone had caused his eyes to narrow. 'Meaning?' he drawled.

'Meaning . . .' defiantly she stared down at him, 'that you don't seem particularly pleased at the moment. Having thought it was such a good idea, now you seem to have gone off it. It just makes me wonder what your motives were.'

Without seeming to move he was standing beside her, his fingers fastened tightly round her wrist. 'My motives are what they have been from the first.' His voice was very smooth and cold. 'It's yours I'm beginning to question.' Abruptly he released his hold as if he found the experience of touching her not to his liking. 'I'm afraid I was so involved with the brilliance of my idea that I didn't enquire too much into your reasons for accepting.'

'Mine are probably similar to your own.' Tension made her clip the words short. 'At least . . .' Her voice faded as she decided that it might be best to leave her thoughts unspoken.

'At least?' he insisted.

'At least, as far as you told me.' Suddenly bold, she faced him without flinching. 'But now I'm beginning to suspect some other reason.'

'But what could that other reason possibly be?' His eyes seemed cold and cruel. 'Except that we suit each other.' You don't imagine, he seemed to be saying to her, that I find you attractive? 'You told me that you weren't in love with anyone and you seemed to have no strong reasons to reject the suggestion. If you had, my dear, then I'm afraid you've left it rather late.' He turned abruptly away from her, the long fingers searching in a box for a thin black cheroot. Victoria watched the match flare as he lit it, then pulled the smoke deep into his lungs before releasing it in one long slow breath.

'It's not too late. There's nothing to prevent me walking out of this house right now.' She saw his head jerk round so that he looked at her through narrowed eyes. 'It would be comparatively easy to put matters right. Easier than if ...' she bit her lower lip nervously, '... if we waited.'

'But you won't do that, will you, Victoria?' A tiny smile appeared at the corner of his mouth. Because then you would look almost as much of a fool as I would. Remember——' He stepped towards her, then realising that he still held the cheroot in one hand, he turned to stub it out impatiently in the large glass ashtray on the table behind him. 'Remember this is our wedding day.' Again he circled her neck with one strong hand so that a shudder ran through her. 'It's been a strain for both

of us, for you more than for me. And I've been a
brute to you.' Although she was aware that this
was the technique she had seen being worked so
often Victoria had no defence against it. 'Will you
forgive me?' She knew she was being manipulated
and could do nothing. He bent his head so he could
kiss her forehead. 'Now,' sliding his hand down,
he pulled her gently towards the telephone, 'tell me
your mother's number. I'll dial it for you and then
you speak to her.'

Victoria watched while his fingers found the
digits she recited, then she looked at him while they
both listened to the ringing tone.

'Hello. Hello.' Instantly she recognised her
mother's voice, although tonight it sounded excited
and full of stress. She held out her hand for the
receiver.

'Hello, Mother.' She strove to keep her voice
light and even.

'Oh, Victoria!' There was a sob in her mother's
voice. 'Thank goodness! I've been trying . . .'

'Hello, Mrs Kendall.' Benedict took the receiver
from Victoria's hand. 'This is Benedict. I'm afraid
Victoria is rather overcome.' He turned away as
his wife tried to control the tears that were
suddenly flowing down her cheeks. 'Now if you're
going to be angry then I hope you'll blame me.
No, no, it was all my fault. I insisted on the secrecy.
She wanted to tell you. Of course I understand.
Yes, I do know. Well, don't worry, you're not
going to be done out of a celebration. We'll be up
to see you as soon as possible and we shall be very
contrite and fit in with whatever plans you have
for us. Yes, naturally, I do know how upset you

and Mr Kendall must feel. Victoria has told me so much about you . . .' He paused, listening, his eyes refusing to respond to the angry scornful expression on her face. 'Yes, and I am too, looking forward to it very much. And now here's Victoria. She's feeling all right again. It's been rather an emotional time for her.' And after a few more smooth words he held out the receiver to Victoria, closing the door of the sitting room silently behind him as he left her to make her peace with her mother.

'You've recovered now, Victoria?' Unexpectedly Benedict put out a hand to cover hers lying on the white tablecloth. At once her heart gave that treacherous bound which was becoming so familiar to her after less than twelve hours of marriage. It cost her an effort not to flinch, to smile with apparent unconcern into those disturbing perceptive eyes.

'Yes.' The word was a sophisticated drawl. 'I'm sorry I was so silly.' She shook her head, aware of her hair moving silkily about her shoulders, seeing his eyes following its cloudy motion. 'I had no intention of acting like a bride. I . . .' Angry that she was unable to control the colour in her cheeks as his eyes came back to hers, she smiled faintly and pulled her hand from beneath his to adjust the narrow strap of her dress. 'I suppose it was hearing my mother's voice, realising just how much of a shock it was for her. After all, when I have a daughter,' the colour in her cheeks deepened when she realised what her inhibitions had made her say, 'I shall hate to hear about her marriage from television.' She flicked her eyes up from the table to look at him defiantly.

They were sitting in one of London's newest, most elegant restaurants, their table apparently specially reserved, set in a tiny alcove which gave them some privacy although they had an un-interrupted view of the room. With a stab of irrita-tion Victoria had wondered when they were shown to their places if perhaps Benedict didn't want anyone to see them. It was the sort of place where he might expect to run into some of his friends from the glossy world he inhabited and she suspec-ted that he might be realising that his wife didn't compare too well with his usual companions, the Baroness in particular.

But she had dismissed that suspicion as un-worthy. Especially when she decided that if they had had the normal kind of marriage such a desire for privacy would have been regarded as absolutely natural. Besides—she remembered that glimpse of herself in the mirror in her bedroom—her appear-ance wasn't all that much of an anti-climax. It was amazing what a difference fine feathers made. Even Benedict had been surprised. She had seen that momentary flash of amazement when she had gone downstairs to join him in the hall before leaving.

Her dress was pink but not the wishy-washy colour usually associated with the name and which she normally avoided. No, this was a vibrant colour, rich and deep with just a hint of golden-brown lurking somewhere underneath the shim-mery material. The bodice was scanty with a deep plunging neckline which showed off the tan she had acquired on an early holiday in the Algarve last month. The skirt was full, but the soft material swirled about her legs and clung tenderly as she moved.

'Would you like to dance, Victoria?' Benedict's invitation interrupted her reverie and before she even realised what she was being asked she heard her voice accepting.

The small group was playing something sweet and old-fashioned and sentimental when he put his arm round her, pulling her inexorably against him, ignoring her slight resistance, or possibly not even noticing it. She wondered if he realised that she was trembling. Or was he so used to his dancing partners showing their reactions to him that it no longer registered? She smiled cynically. Then when the music stopped while the players selected another tune she pretended to think the dance had finished and turned to make her way back to the table.

'No, you don't!' His fingers closed like steel round her wrist and turned her back to him. He was smiling, but underneath the surface she could see that he was tense and perhaps a little angry. 'I'm not letting you off so lightly.' And his hands linked about her waist, holding her firmly against him while they moved in time to some Latin-American rhythm, pulsating, throbbing, exciting.

Victoria felt ripples starting at the base of her spine and trembling through her body as she looked up into his face. Although she smiled she felt that she was merely baring her teeth at him, in a subconscious futile attempt to warn him off. But he continued to incline his head towards her with every indication of devotion, perhaps even passion.

Victoria leaned against him, allowing her face to touch his for a moment. She felt the very faint rasp of his recently shaven cheek, smelled the unusual distinctive cologne which was so familiar to her. She spoke softly into his ear so that none of the other dancers could hear.

'Is this simply for my benefit?' Her tone was only slightly waspish. 'Or is there someone here you want to impress?'

'Victoria.' His laugh was deep and throbbing as if she had said something terribly witty just for his ears alone. 'Darling.' The music ended, but he refused to release her, apparently oblivious of the other dancers who were drifting back to their tables. Only when he heard his name spoken did Benedict look up in surprise and with a reluctance which was almost genuine enough to deceive Victoria.

'Ben! I knew it was you. I told you so, didn't I?' Victoria watched Jeremy Ransome turn to the tall bored blonde who was standing looking into the mid-distance. 'Didn't I, Tanya?'

'Yes.' Without taking her eyes from whatever was attracting her attention Tanya agreed with him.

'And Miss Kendall too.' Having got the confirmation he wanted Jeremy turned his attention to the other girl. 'Well,' with a sly little glance in Benedict's direction, 'I suppose I'd better call you Mrs Gabriell now.'

'Yes, you'd better. Or even Victoria. That's her name, you know.' Benedict smiled as if undisturbed at this unexpected meeting with an old acquaintance and with his hand on Victoria's elbow guided her firmly in the direction of their table, Jeremy with his partner trailing after followed them.

'I was saying to Tanya, when we saw you on the box, that you could have knocked me down with a feather. He always was a dark horse—I told you that, didn't I, Tanya?' And this time, without waiting for her confirmation, he stood smiling down at them, watching while Benedict held Victoria's chair and then slipped into his own. 'But to marry your secretary!' He waved an apologetic hand at Victoria explaining that he was joking. 'It's not what we expected from you, old man.'

Victoria looked at him with a dislike she had always felt but had until now striven to conceal. It seemed funny to think that this fattish man with thinning blond hair had been at school with Benedict, who looked quite ten years his junior. She glanced across at her husband and saw the familiar spark of irritation in his eyes. He smiled in that tight polite way which indicated that an explosion of rage was imminent.

'Yes, but as you say, I never did do what was expected of me. And as you know, we were married this afternoon and at the moment we're enjoying each other's company.' He put out his hand took Victoria's and this time she didn't withdraw it.

'Of course, old chap.' Jeremy winked ponderously and turning to his girl-friend put a possessive hand on her arm. 'We're de trop here, Tanya old girl—interrupting the honeymoon. Goodbye,' he whispered fatuously as he led her away.

Victoria stared at Benedict's hand linked so casually round hers, saw the long dark fingers, the sprinkling of fine hair on the back of the hand, the bracelet of the thin gold watch under the gleaming white cuff, and again she felt the sting of tears at the back of her eyes.

'Sorry I forgot to tell you, Ben old son.' Jeremy was standing beside their table again, still whispering, apparently imagining this in some mysterious way made his presence less intrusive. 'I forgot to say that I've just come back from New York and two nights ago I was with Camilla. She'll be so surprised . . .' He smiled again turned and tiptoed ponderously back to his own table. Victoria's eyes moved from Jeremy across to the grim man sitting opposite her, unaware that her lashes were glinting with tears. She hadn't had long to wait until the baleful shadow of Camilla Kertesz began to stretch out over them.

'Shall we go?' Benedict's voice was as hard and relentless as his eyes. Then with an obvious effort, a tiny shrug of his shoulders, 'If you would like to, that is, Victoria.'

And of course she had agreed. She sat beside him in the car as it nosed its way along the busy streets, only once casting a tentative glance at the stern profile as he brooded silently over his driving. She knew that she daren't speak. If she did she would only burst into tears. And that would probably tell him that she was as unhappy as he was.

But when they reached the house—it was too early for her to think of it as home—she had waited until he had closed the door of the garage and walked with him through the long garden towards the back door. Inside she had stood rather aimlessly before moving tentatively towards the staircase, where his voice had halted her.

'I told Lumsden to leave some coffee in the sitting-room. I suppose we might as well drink it.'

Victoria followed him, filled with resentment at the peremptory manner which reminded her of that first day she had gone to his office. She stood in the doorway, still undecided, wishing she could find the courage to snap some remark at him and walk firmly upstairs.

'Well, come in.' He glanced round from the small table where the coffee had been left on a small hotplate, then turned, holding out a cup towards her.

Victoria stepped into the room, took the steaming coffee and walked across to the huge window. There had been a weariness in his attitude that clutched at her, making her realise that perhaps the day had been as much of a strain for him as for her.

'Victoria.'

'Yes.' She softened towards him as she was afraid she always would. 'Yes?' She turned and put down her empty cup.

'I bought this for you.' He was holding a small box in his hand. 'I thought this would be the best time to give it to you.' He shrugged and smiled at himself. 'Maybe I was wrong.'

'What is it?'

'Open it and see.'

She took the small blue leather box and pressed the tiny gilt stud. 'Oh, Benedict!' She stared down at the diamond gleaming on the bed of dark velvet.

'It's an engagement ring,' he explained unnecessarily. 'I thought you should have one.'

'It's beautiful!'

'Try it on.'

'Yes, of course.' She laughed as she took it out and slipped it on to her finger beside the gleaming new broad gold band. 'It's perfect!' She extended her hand so that he could admire it. 'Thank you.'

'I wasn't sure of your taste. I thought that was a safe bet.'

'Yes.' Deliberately she tried to echo his unemotional tone. 'A nice big diamond is usually a good bet.'

'I'm sorry.' He grinned, suddenly disarming and boyish. 'I didn't mean to sound so banal. Put it down to lack of experience.'

Laughing up into that handsome, slightly menacing face, Victoria suddenly caught her breath and wished—how she wished!—that perhaps she had made a mistake. After all, maybe Benedict hadn't meant that their marriage should be such a formality. Perhaps in a subconscious effort to protect herself against disappointment she had back at the beginning decided that was what he had in mind. But if she had been wrong. Her mind spun giddily, for a moment intoxicated with the possibility, and then his voice broke in, shattering her dream harshly.

'Well, I imagine you're dying to go to bed, Victoria.' She looked up at him through long sooty lashes, saw the way he pushed his fingers through the long dark hair. 'I know I feel absolutely whacked.'

'Yes, of course.' Abruptly, determined to show nothing of her hurt, she turned for the door. 'Goodnight.' Her voice was the cool Miss Kendall's.

'Goodnight, Victoria.' The gentleness of his voice did not penetrate her self-protective veneer.

'I'm sorry the day has been such a strain for you.' She closed the door gently behind her and ran swiftly up the flight of shallow curving steps to her bedroom. And only when she had turned the key in her door did she allow herself the luxury and relief of permitting her own misery to wash away in a storm of silent weeping.

CHAPTER THREE

IT was surprising how easy it was to settle down to the routine of driving to the office with Benedict, doing exactly what she had been doing for eight years and then driving home with him in the evening. In fact, life continued much as it always had done, except for that little while between going home at night and arriving in the office.

Benedict had suggested, tentatively for Benedict Gabriell, that perhaps she would prefer to give up work. He had come into the dining room that first morning slightly surprised at finding her there ahead of him, presiding over the coffee things and had, after a few rustlings of *The Times*, looked at her over the top of the sheet.

'Maybe, Victoria . . .' perhaps something in her expression made him hesitate, '. . . maybe you'd rather give up work now. There's no need for you to continue, you know, if . . .'

'Is that what you want?' The coldness of her tone was an echo of the way she had answered his greeting when he had come into the room.

'Of course not.' He turned a page irritably and sighed. 'Of course I don't mean that. It's entirely up to you. I just thought that perhaps you'd enjoy being at home for a bit—I don't know.'

'I think I should prefer going to the office.' She stirred her cup with an air of concentration. 'There's your programme in two weeks and I don't think anyone else could cope with that at such short notice. Besides, I don't think there would be enough for me to do at home. Lumsden seems to have everything firmly under control.' Her tone did nothing to conceal the almost instant dislike she had taken to the man.

'Yes, he's very efficient.' Benedict was apparently oblivious of her feelings. 'And as you say, it wouldn't be easy to find a replacement at such short notice.' If he was very relieved at her decision he was able to appear casual about it. 'Oh, and I think we should arrange to go down to Cornwall next weekend. We could leave on Friday after lunch and come back on Monday morning.'

'All right.' She got up and began to collect the breakfast things together before she remembered there was no need for her to do that. 'And what about Harrogate? When shall we be able to go up there?'

'Well,' he appeared to consider, 'shall we say in three weeks? I'm afraid we'll have to wait till the recording is made. It's all going to be something of a rush.' There was a mild complaint in his voice which she decided to ignore.

The week went calmly, if anything in that office could be said to be calm. There was the usual almost non-stop ringing of the telephone as the studios called to demand briefs on the form of the programme and then shocked protests when they learned that Benedict was going to be unavailable from Friday till Monday. And there was a frantic call from the publishers, who were worried about the possible repercussions of Benedict's criticism of a South American government in his latest book.

It was all fairly typical, and from time to time Victoria had to pinch herself in an effort to remember that she was no longer simply Benedict's secretary. And he did little to help by his occasional abstracted requests to, 'Call the studios and tell them, Miss Kendall, that I can't agree to another change of format,' or, 'Use your fatal charm, Miss Kendall.' Once or twice he caught himself up and used her Christian name, but it was apparently only too easy for him to slip into the old boss-secretary relationship once they left the enforced intimacy of Peverell Square.

And there was no doubt life in his home could be very pleasant. If Victoria could ignore the antipathy which existed between Lumsden and herself she might almost have been happy living there. It was a beautiful house, one which gave her constant pleasure, especially after the rather anonymous furnished flats she had been used to.

Her bedroom had been a surprise, for she had imagined something rather austere and even anonymous, the spare bedroom of a typical bachelor. Not, she reminded herself even as the thought struck her, that Benedict was that. And there was almost the suggestion of a woman's hand in the choice of furnishings, although there was nothing in the least pretty-pretty about the room.

It was a charming bedroom, the kind she had dreamed all her life of having, and by chance the pale Wedgwood green of the walls was one of her favourite colours, picked up again in the deep velvety pile of the plain carpet. The curtains hung in smooth chintzy folds from ceiling to floor and a touch of a button made them close with a swish

over the wide french windows which opened on to
the tiny balcony. The same rose-strewn material
with trailing green leaves was repeated in the bed-
cover and the padded headboard. By the window,
where she could sit and look out on the garden,
was a small chair covered in pink silk.

Against one wall a small Regency side table
served as a desk, the colour of its smooth golden
wood picked up in the expensive modern units
which covered the opposite wall. The high doors
opened to reveal an extravagant range of cupboards and shelves, enough space to satisfy the
most fashion-conscious woman and which Victoria
feared she would never be able to fill adequately.

Behind one of the doors a small bathroom was
concealed, papered to match the curtains in the
bedroom and with the suite in the subtle colour of
green which she liked so much. Piles of towels in
various shades of pink and a row of pink jars
holding bath salts and essences added a few more
luxurious touches.

In the fourth wall of her bedroom, gleaming
white like all the paintwork, was the door which
led into Benedict's room. She could sit in bed and
watch it, could see the brass bolt slipped firmly
across just as she imagined the one on the other
side to be. To protect them from each other. She
had never been in his bedroom, never ventured
through that door flanked by carefully chosen
flower prints. Benedict had shown her to her room
on that first day—checking to see that it reached
the required standard for a new wife, she thought
cynically—but he hadn't offered to let her see his
room. Nevertheless she had glimpsed it once or

twice when she had passed the open door on the landing and had been surprised to notice that it was smaller than her own, with the mahogany top of a single bed clearly visible in the reflection from the mirror. Its colours were striking but rather sombre with deep brown walls, except for the one behind the bed which was papered with surrealist brown roses on a cream background and just a hint of orange here and there.

Lumsden had shown her the rest of the house at Benedict's request, but with the grudging manner that characterised all their dealings when they were alone together, letting her know all too clearly that he would not tolerate her presence in the kitchen.

'If you want anything, madam, I wish you would ring.' He had returned from his flatlet above the garage to find her making a cup of instant coffee. Victoria, guiltily aware of his disapproval, had jumped, spilling some water on the immaculate blue and white tiling which he immediately began to mop up in a patient way.

'I've certainly no intention, Lumsden,' she tried to speak lightly, 'of calling you from your flat to make me a cup of coffee.'

'Nevertheless, madam,' he regarded her smiling face sourly, 'I should prefer it.' He paused. 'It is usual in these families, madam.'

Victoria tried to control her irritation. 'Nevertheless, Lumsden, I shall do what I like in my own home.'

'I don't think Lumsden approves of me going near his precious kitchen.' In spite of her determination to take the matter lightly, she felt tense when she tried to speak to Benedict about the matter later that evening.

'Oh?' He frowned as he looked up from the pile of notes she had typed out for him during the day, then with the same abstracted manner he returned his attention to his notes, 'I shouldn't worry, he'll come round. Don't let him bully you. It's what you say that goes, after all.'

'I don't think he approves of me at all. It's not just the kitchen. He never unbends.'

'Hmm, yes, he is a bit of a cold fish.'

'Do you . . .' Victoria swallowed nervously, 'do you really think we need someone full-time? Living in, I mean?'

That at least got his full attention, for he put down his papers and looked at her with the same air of patience sorely tried that she had seen on Lumsden's face such a short time before. 'Look, Victoria, it's up to you to try and get on with Lumsden. Of course I'll support you in any little battles you two might have, but try to remember how difficult it is to get any help here. And be thankful. If he gives us notice heaven knows where we'd find anyone else. I was very lucky to find a replacement as soon as the Jacksons left. If it hadn't been for . . .' He broke off and frowned again, tapping the end of his pen rapidly against one palm in a way that told her he was feeling very irritated. 'If it hadn't been for . . . a friend I would never have found anyone half as efficient. The agencies are flooded with requests for people like him.' He looked down at the papers in his hands in a way that clearly asked to be left in peace.

'Then I'll try,' Victoria got up and walked to the

door, 'not to annoy him.' She spoke sarcastically,
coldly. 'I can see only too clearly what you mean. He
would be so much more difficult to replace than . . .'
She had been meaning to say 'than a wife', but she
bit off the words and contented herself with closing
the door in an unusually forceful fashion.

But now she could forget Lumsden for a few days
as they were on their way down to Cornwall for
the weekend, to meet Mrs Gabriell to see if she
approved of her new daughter-in-law. And as if to
put her in the mood, Benedict was at his most
charming as they drove away from London, leaving
the office at eleven, so, he insisted, that they could
have a leisurely lunch at a pub he knew and could
forget all the hassle of the last day or two.

Even as she sardonically noticed that he was
trying out the old magic again, Victoria knew that
it was working, felt all her tensions ease away as
she lay back in her seat and smiled in response to
some small joke he had made. She was as foolish
as all the other women in his life, just as ready to
forgive his moods and explosive temper, to make
excuses for him.

She imagined he had been used to it all his life.
Probably his mother was the same. It was strange
that she had never met Benedict's mother, who had
come up several times to London in the years since
she had been his secretary. But always his obsession
for keeping the two parts of his life separate had
been successful. She had invariably made the rail
bookings, of course. But never once had Mrs
Gabriell come up to the office and Benedict had
never asked Victoria to go to the station to pick up

the visitor as he often did with business associates. And now he had decided to mix them up with a vengeance. There were no half measures about the man.

'Are you feeling nervous?' The yellow eyes were looking at her curiously as she wakened from her reverie to see him tipping some more wine into her glass.

'Nervous?' She played for time, watching him take the glass of lager to his lips, saw the tip of his tongue remove a trace of froth, then a familiar knowing twist of his mouth.

'Yes, Miss Kendall.' His mockery was gentle for once. 'Aren't most girls nervous about meeting their mother-in-law for the first time?'

'I suppose they are.' Victoria gulped at the wine and felt it deep and warm inside her. 'And most girls have the opportunity of breaking them in to the idea that they are running off with their sons.' The implication of what she had said struck her, causing a blush to spread across her cheeks. 'I've been thrown in at the deep end.'

'I don't think you need worry.' His voice was the deep comforting one known so intimately to the viewing public, and surprisingly his hand came out to cover hers as it lay on the white cloth. The large diamond of her ring cut painfully into her finger, but she scarcely noticed. 'I think you're the kind of daughter-in-law whom most mothers would approve of.'

'Ouch!' Victoria, affected by the wine, determined to be lighthearted and daring. 'I don't know if that's a compliment. It sounds so stodgy and dull!'

His lips curved into the slow, almost reluctant smile which could be so devastating when used. Victoria recognised it at once, but to her dismay her defences on this occasion seemed slow to react. She felt the tremor at the base of her spine envelop her entire body as his thumb moved idly, tingling against the palm of her hand. 'I didn't mean that.' His words scarcely penetrated her bemused thoughts.

'Didn't you?' Her eyes were on his mouth, her mind in the heavens.

'No, in fact I ought to have told you earlier. You look particularly attractive this morning. It's new, isn't it?'

'What?' She withdrew her hand as the waitress put plates in front of them. 'Oh, this.' She looked down at the cream silk blouse and the linen pants in beige overchecked with green. 'Yes, I got it as a concession to the country. I didn't know what the weather would be like. And I'd been meaning to buy myself a new velvet jacket for some time . . .' She looked up at the girl who was offering herbed new potatoes to go with the grilled trout. 'Yes, just a few, thank you.' She sat back and smiled, watching the intense interest shown by the waitress in the man she was serving.

'You suit green, do you know that?' When the girl had moved reluctantly away from their table Benedict returned to the subject, passing her the salt and pepper while he studied her closely through slightly narrowed eyes.

'Oh, I don't know about that.' She tried to repress the absurd spasm of pleasure that shot through her. 'I've always liked it. And,' she paused, feeling gauche and shy, emotions which she had thought outgrown, 'and that's one of the things I like so much about my bedroom—the colours are just about the ones I would have chosen myself. And the rest of the house too,' she babbled, disconcerted by his gaze, 'you really have a lovely place, Benedict.'

'We,' he interrupted her with a return of his familiar hauteur, as if he had decided that she had had enough indulgence for the time being. She looked at him blankly so that he explained again, still coldly, '*We* have a lovely place.' Then with a sigh he looked down at his plate. 'I'm glad you approve.' He spoke wearily, but for once she couldn't tell whether or not he was being sarcastic.

By the time they were on the road again he seemed completely to have recovered from his momentary moodiness and was putting himself out to be specially agreeable and amusing. But then he switched on the radio, twirled the knobs till he had found a station sending out quiet music and advised her to go to sleep.

Victoria yawned approving the suggestion. 'I think the wine has made me sleepy.' She half-turned towards him, nestling down in the seat. 'Are you sure you don't want me to drive for a bit?'

'No.' He cast a sardonic glance down towards her. 'After what you just said I doubt I'd be able to relax. You know I don't approve of drink and driving.'

'Of course I know.' Her laugh was soft and sleepy. 'But you needn't sound so smug about it. Remember you did have lager with your meal.'

'Mmm, I think I can manage to cope with half a

pint. But now,' reaching over to the back seat he pulled over a soft mohair rug which he handed to her, 'tuck yourself up in that. And don't snore, it upsets my equilibrium.'

'Of course I won't snore. What a suggestion!' She pulled the rug about her legs.

'Well, I think they must have started up a saw-mill in the room through the wall from mine.'

'How can you . . .' Victoria smiled to herself as she drifted dreamily for a moment, but she didn't finish her sentence, because a sudden thought had swept all others out of her mind. What, she wondered, was Mrs Gabriell going to think when she found out that her son and his brand new wife didn't even occupy the same bedroom?

'We're almost there, Victoria.' Benedict's deep tones brought her back from the dreamless sleep she had enjoyed for the last part of the journey and she struggled up as they approached a small village in time for her to read the name Penmorra as Benedict slowed to take a lane leading off to the left.

'You should have warned me.' Suddenly her heart was thumping and her throat was dry.

'I thought I just had.' Beneath the teasing note she wondered if perhaps he felt as tense and uptight as she did herself, but her searching glance told her nothing. 'Worried?' Briefly he took his attention away from the road, pleasing her by reaching out his hand to squeeze hers comfortingly.

'No, of course not.' But her voice sounded so weak and unconvincing that she laughed. 'Well, perhaps a bit.'

'Don't be.' He returned his attention to a sudden

left-hand turn through a wide gate and withdrew his hand to negotiate a drive curving along under a hedge of tall rhododendrons blazing with huge salmon pink flowers.

'Benedict,' impulsively she wound down her window, 'how absolutely gorgeous!' She turned towards him in a swirl of gold-brown hair, her eyes shining with pleasure. 'What an incredible colour!'

'I didn't want to tell you about them in case we missed them,' he told her. 'Quite often by the first week in June they're almost over, but I suppose the cold weather early on delayed them. They're my mother's pride and joy, so if you admire them you'll be half-way there.' As he spoke he turned another corner so that suddenly a wide green lawn dropped away on their left towards the sea and on their right, sheltered on the landward side by some tall elms, lay Trezance. Victoria had only a moment to admire the long low lines of the building, the way the clinging vines had been clipped neatly at the end of the house and allowed to creep just a little way round to the south-facing front, before the door opened and a tall grey-haired, pretty woman came running down the few steps and opening the door of the car.

'Mother!' Victoria was still fiddling with her seat-belt when Benedict enveloped his mother in a warm hug. She noticed how his voice lost its habitually mocking tone when he spoke to her. 'You look well. Now come and meet your daughter-in-law.'

A moment later, Victoria felt her hands being held tightly while two surprisingly blue eyes looked at her very intensely indeed.

'Victoria.' There was a shade of relief in the voice

as she felt a soft cheek pressed against hers. 'How very pleased I am to see you, my dear. You're quite different from the picture I had in my mind.'

'Come, Mother.' Benedict's voice was mildly reproving. 'The television pictures were clear enough.'

'Well, it was difficult to see properly.' Mrs Gabriell wrinkled her nose at her son. 'And besides, I was in a state of shock at the time.' She put a friendly arm round Victoria and drew her round the car in the direction of the door. 'Now come and meet Janet—she's been as anxious and impatient to meet you as I have. Ben will have told you all about her.'

Janet, who was hovering inside the front door, was clearly the Cornish equivalent of Lumsden—and, decided Victoria, looking at her shy smiling face and rosy cheeks, a great improvement.

'Now then, Benedict!' Janet brushed a hand against the dark cheek reprovingly. 'You had no right to spring such a surprise on us. Your mother and I are too old for such things. But,' as she took Victoria's hand and held it she looked at her consideringly, 'maybe you've done something sensible. For once,' she added discouragingly.

'You think so, Janet?' As he smiled at his wife over the heads of the two older women one eye closed in a meaning wink.

'Yes, I do. I'm very pleased to meet you, Mrs Benedict. And now you'll be ready for some tea, so I'll just go to the kitchen and make it. Maybe your mother will show you up to your room. I got the front bedroom ready for you.'

'You see who's boss here!' As the kitchen door swung closed behind Janet Mrs Gabriell led Victoria towards the stairs. 'I'm afraid we all have to do what we're told. Will you go and bring up your cases, darling?' She spoke to Benedict, who was still standing in the middle of the oak strip floor of the hall and without waiting for a reply she continued to climb the stairs, her hand firmly on Victoria's elbow.

'This is what Janet means by the front room.' Mrs Gabriell pushed open a door on the top landing, but instead of finding herself in a bedroom as she had expected, Victoria saw they had to go down a few more steps before they reached a large room with bare floorboards which gleamed with generations of wax polishing, scattered here and there with fleecy cream rugs. 'We usually keep it for guests as it's so convenient, with its own bathroom next door. And it seemed more appropriate . . .' She broke off with a smile when she saw the colour come into the girl's cheeks, then turned as they heard firm footsteps on the wooden floor of the corridor.

'Well, I'll leave you.' Benedict's mother smiled at Victoria as she walked to the door, pausing briefly to touch her son's hand as he put down their cases on a bench just inside the door. 'I think I agree with Janet—you've done something very sensible.' And she went out, closing the door very gently behind her.

Benedict stood for a moment, hands on his hips, staring across at Victoria, who had put out a hand to grasp one of the heavy wood posts at the foot of the large high double bed. She found it impossible to withdraw her eyes from his no matter how much she longed to turn casually away and walk over to where the net curtains were billowing softly in the warm breeze from the open window. He looked so vital in the casual checked jacket and open-necked shirt, and there was a spark of something in those enigmatic eyes that she couldn't identify. It might have been his usual cynical challenging look, but she didn't think so.

But as if he too were conscious of some potent force stretching between them he turned deliberately away, slipping the jacket from his shoulders and tossing it carelessly on to the white counterpane. In relief Victoria looked away from him, a few quick steps taking her to the window where she stood taking gulps of fresh salty air. Beneath her, where the swathe of lawn reached the shore, she could see the waves ripple and glitter in the sun of the late afternoon.

By the time she heard a step behind her the hammering of her heart had eased, the dryness had gone from her mouth so that she was able to speak in a normal tone.

'It's a beautiful situation, Benedict,' she said brightly. 'I didn't know it would be so near the sea.' She waited for him to answer, but when he didn't swung round to look at him enquiringly. He was paying no attention to the beauty of the scene that lay before him, instead his eyes seemed to be concentrated on her, looking at her with that slightly narrowed assessing gaze which she knew only too well and had learned to respect. She drew a sharp breath, putting her hand to her throat in a betraying little gesture of self-protection as she tried again. 'Why didn't you tell me?' she smiled nervously.

'Do you agree with them?' He ignored the conversation she had been trying to generate and spoke softly, at the same time raising one hand and running it down the curve of her cheek.

'Agree?' Her voice trembled dangerously. 'I don't understand.'

'No?' The yellow eyes narrowed still further, and this time she recognised disbelief. There was a long pause while she tried to control the trembling that his continued touch on her face brought. 'Do you agree with my mother and with Janet? That in marrying you,' his fingers moved to her throat, 'I did something very sensible?'

Victoria stared up at him, the slanted brown eyes determined to be controlled and wary. 'Of course.' She tried to be lighthearted and it was almost a laugh that issued from her lips. 'Do you expect me to disagree? I think Janet hit the nail right on the head.'

There was no response to the feeble joke and she wondered if he had even heard what she said. But at last she saw his lips move, heard that deep fascinating voice. 'And you, Victoria my sweet? Were you being sensible?'

'I . . . I don't know.'

He did laugh then, but he didn't sound the least bit amused. But then his hands moved, linking themselves about her slender waist, pulling her against him so that she felt the length of his body strong and hard against hers. 'You don't know,' he jeered. 'Here we are alone together in this beautiful situation,' he mocked her words wickedly and swung her round so that together they looked across at the large inviting bed, 'and with nothing to do but please each other.' His mouth came down to hers, searching and fierce and determined to dominate. For a moment she softened against him, all her resistance undermined by the unexpected swirl of pleasure that his kiss had brought, the whirling maelstrom of joy and desire that swept through her. But then her good sense reasserted itself, as she remembered exactly the kind of relationship he had chosen for them. It was too late for him to change the rules now simply because he found it convenient. Angrily she dragged herself away from him, away from the cruel possessiveness of his mouth.

'Damn you!' She glared up at him and pressed her fingers to her mouth. 'Leave me alone!'

Instead of being angry as she had expected he put back his head and laughed. 'So you aren't all cool self-control, Miss Kendall. Surprising.' He dropped his hands from her waist and stepped back, the smile fading slowly from his face as he surveyed her. 'But you needn't worry, you're quite safe. Even tonight when we have to share that double bed,' he jerked his head backwards, 'I shall take great care not to disturb you.' Abruptly he turned away from her and walked to the door. 'But now I suggest we go down, otherwise Mother and Janet may think that I'm tasting forbidden fruits. Not that they would know they are forbidden, of course. I shall wait for you at the top of the stairs,' he bowed mockingly as he hesitated with the door knob in his hand, 'so that we can present the picture expected of honeymooners.' The solid wood door closed firmly behind him.

'Did you bring a swimming costume with you, Victoria?' They were sitting in the small dining room to the left of the front door with the floor-length sash window thrown open to the soft evening air. They had just finished the simple perfect meal which Janet had served and eaten with them and were chatting idly over coffee which they had decided to drink at the table. All three pairs of female eyes seemed to be drawn towards Benedict, who sat with one arm crooked over the back of his dining chair while he sipped a brandy and puffed contentedly at a cheroot.

'I'm sorry, Helen,' Victoria dragged her eyes away from his face when she realised that some sort of reply was expected by her mother-in-law.

'I was asking you . . .' it was difficult for Victoria to avoid blushing at the knowing, amused look Helen Gabriell sent across the round polished table towards Janet, 'whether you brought a swimming costume. The weather is so perfect at the moment it seems a pity not to make the most of it.'

'Yes, I did. Benedict,' Victoria fluttered her eyelashes at him in a way she hoped would annoy him while promoting the deception of the entranced lovers, 'Benedict told me that perhaps there would be a chance of swimming in the sea. He didn't tell me you could open a garden gate and step straight into the water.'

'I'm beginning to wonder exactly what he did tell you.' Janet got up and began to collect the dishes. 'You don't seem to know very much about us.' Victoria wondered if the reproof in the woman's voice was for her more than for Benedict.

'Well, you see,' she spoke indulgently, teasingly, aware that the wine she had drunk with the meal had loosened her tongue, 'he always had this thing about his secretaries. His last one told me—oh, she was called Janet too, by the way.' From the corner of her eye she saw that his lips had tightened, the eyes had narrowed slightly, and suddenly nervous, she jumped up, making a great fuss about collecting some small dishes from the centre of the table and carrying them over to Janet's tray on the sideboard. 'But you must let me help you, Janet, after that lovely meal I insist on doing some of the washing up.'

'You can insist as much as you like, I won't let you touch anything.' To emphasise the refusal Janet sat down in her chair again. 'Besides, we're dying, Mrs Gabriell and I, to hear what Janet—this other Janet—told you about Ben.'

Weakly Victoria subsided into her seat, trying to avoid looking across the table.

'Go on.' Mrs Gabriell was amused. 'You can't stop a story half way through, my dear.' She lowered her voice. 'What did Janet tell you? Just ignore his glowering.' She laughed across at her son.

Victoria took a deep breath. 'She told me that he got so fed-up with his secretaries breathing hot passion over him that he treated them all with severe detachment, giving no hint of his private life in the office and generally acting the martinet. In fact behaving so boorishly that no one in their right mind could fancy him in the least.'

'Oh dear!' Mrs Gabriell's sigh was betrayed by

the sparkle in her eyes. 'And to think that I always imagined that the man I saw on television was the real Benedict, the only one, in fact.'

'Don't you believe it, Helen.' Now that she was able to see a faint smile at the corner of his mouth Victoria felt she was enjoying herself. 'The first time I went to the office he practically ordered me from the place, accused me of inefficiency, flightiness, juvenility and other things I'm too polite to mention here.'

'Well,' Janet rose from her seat again and went across to the sideboard and lifted the tray, 'I'm glad we know now. And all these years we've been thinking . . .' She shook her head at Benedict, who had risen to open the door for her, and walked heavily through with a smile on her lips.

'Now, I'm going to do the washing up with Janet,' Helen spoke to her son, 'and you're going to take Victoria for a stroll round the garden. I always think it's something special in the twilight on a summer's night and if you go along the drive you'll get the scent of the rhododendrons quite strongly. Now off you go. You've both had a long drive and you must be ready for bed.' She ushered them ahead of her, across the hall and towards the front door.

Victoria felt Benedict's hand on her arm in a possessive gesture which was solely for his mother's benefit, and to add to the general impression of felicity she leaned her head gently against him. This little meaningless movement was something that she almost instantly regretted when she saw the sudden glitter of tears in Helen's eyes.

'Oh, I'm being silly.' Laughing at herself, Helen

brushed an embarrassed hand across her cheek. 'I'm getting sentimental in my old age!' Leaning forward, she hugged first Victoria and then Benedict, whose arm went round her, holding her against him for a few minutes.

'Isn't it strange, Victoria,' Helen spoke shakily, 'just how innocent these sophisticated men can be!' She grinned up at her son, all her emotionalism disappearing as she recalled what Victoria had said to them. 'Any woman could have told you, Benedict, that if you really wanted to discourage your secretaries you were going about it absolutely the wrong way. Being a brute to them was exactly how to have them all eating out of your hand. But I've no doubt that Victoria has confessed as much to you already. Now I'm going to say goodnight. Will you lock up, Ben, before you go upstairs?' And without waiting for an answer Mrs Gabriell turned and hurried back to the kitchen, leaving the other two staring at each other.

CHAPTER FOUR

HELEN had been right about the rhododendrons. As they walked along the drive to the road in the dusk the scent, rich and aromatic seemed to hang heavy on the air, but Victoria scarcely noticed. Her mind was too involved with the words Helen had spoken as they stood in the hall by the open front door. Was it possible that Benedict might put two and two together and understand what surely must have puzzled him even a little? Would he realise what her motive had been for marrying?

They strolled silently along the overhung path, each occupied with secret thoughts, separated by more than the yard they seemed determined to keep between them as they went along. At the gate they paused for a moment, looking down towards the sea where one or two small boats bobbed up and down on the tide. Then still without speaking they turned, walking back towards the house.

'Are you cold, Victoria?' His words penetrated the aching nostalgia of her mind and she looked up in bewilderment.

'Cold? No, why?'

'You shivered. I wondered if you might be cold, with your bare arms?'

'No.' She remembered shivering. 'It was a web— a spider's web caught at my throat. I've always been nervous of spiders.'

'Oh.' He seemed to have lost interest and walked

on, allowing her to follow him across the lawn until
they reached the few stone steps and the wooden
gate that led direct from the garden on to the
beach. He sighed then instinctively put out a hand
to help her safely across the path, dropping it when
they crossed the grass towards the belt of trees at
the far end of the house.

'This is the summerhouse.' He led her to a small
white-painted building which had been hidden
from the house by a clump of bushes. He reached
up to the roof of the wooden hut and fumbled
behind one of the fancy scrolls decorating the front.
'Here it is.' He held up what she could just discern
as a key and for a moment his teeth gleamed
triumphantly.

'One step up,' he advised as the door swung open
on its hinges. Inside Victoria could just make out
the shape of two chairs, a small round table and
against the back wall a long old-fashioned sofa. 'I
used this as a den when I was a boy. Three of us
used to gather here and plan the things that kids
usually plan. Sit down.' He hooked one of the
chairs round with one foot. 'I think it'll be clean
enough.'

Victoria did as she was told, smoothing the skirt
of her dress under her as she sat. There was silence
for a little while. She sat looking through the glass
front of the summerhouse, trying to imagine
Benedict as a little boy with his two friends, planning all kinds of escapades, wondering what they
would do when they grew up.

'And what about the others?' It was she who at
last broke the silence.

'The others?' He spoke abstractedly.

'The other two boys. What are they doing now?'

'Oh.' He seemed to relax, to come back from wherever his thoughts had taken him. 'Dave Trevithick is abroad somewhere flying helicopters for a Middle Eastern prince, but Brian is still about—running the family firm in Truro now. They're boatbuilders, and sometimes he takes it into his head to sail round the point there and drop in for tea with Mother and Janet. He has a Jolly Roger which he runs up specially when he knows I'm home, to remind us of the old days when we used to let our imaginations run away with us.' He grinned suddenly. 'I'd like you to meet him.' Then as if regretting his spontaneity he levered himself away from the door arch where he had been leaning. 'Come on then, I see that Mother and Janet have gone upstairs.' He looked towards the top storey of the house where two windows were illuminated with curtains pulled across. 'I'd better see to it that you get inside safely.'

'What do you mean?' She got up and began to walk with him across the lawn, feeling the faint dampness of the grass through her open sandals.

'I mean, my sweet, that I shall make myself scarce for you tonight. That threat I made upstairs . . . I didn't really mean it. I suppose I was merely reverting to type, you know, boorish and awkward.'

'But,' Victoria ignored the taunt, 'but where are you going? You can't . . . you can't use your old room. It's next to Janet's, isn't it? She'd hear you.'

'Don't get so uptight, my sweet.' He really *was* reverting to type, she thought, with his sarcastic tone. 'I shall use the summerhouse. It came to me in a flash as soon as I found the key. It used to be my greatest treat when I was a boy, and I don't see why it shouldn't be still. And I'll be up and about before anyone has a notion of what I've been doing. And you can have the comfort of that large virginal bed for yourself, my dear.'

Victoria's ears were filled with the sound of her own heart hammering as they stood there just outside the circle of light spilling from the front door. In the half-dark Benedict's eyes gleamed strangely so that she had the curious totally irrational feeling that he wanted her to say something, to suggest that perhaps after all they ought to spend the night in the same room. But of course she couldn't, wouldn't risk the jeering refusal, the taunting rejection that would be likely to follow such a suggestion. The lacerations caused by his cutting words were too fresh and deep for that.

With an effort she made herself speak, calmly, forcing all expression from her features as well as her voice. 'If that's what you want. But I would have thought that the sofa which might have been totally adequate when you were a boy would be less comfortable now. However, it's your choice . . .' She turned to go into the house, but as she did so she felt her arm grasped and she was turned again, none too gently, to face him.

'Don't go like that.' His teeth gleamed in a savage little grin, the yellow eyes glowed. 'Not like that, my sweet.' He pulled her against him, holding her close, his cheek faintly rough rasping against her skin in a tingling, disturbing sensation. 'Keep still.' The strength of his arms controlled her attempt to struggle as he spoke into the cloudiness

of her hair. 'Janet has come to pull back the curtains and we mustn't disappoint her.'

Victoria lay still against him for a moment,
almost enjoying the sensation of his mouth against
her skin and hair. But when she decided that no
one took that long to fix curtains she pulled herself
away from him with a firmness that wasn't resisted.
'Finished?' she asked coolly, trying to ignore the
triumph in his smile. 'Goodnight.' And with a whirl
of skirts she turned from him and ran lightly up
the steps across the hall, up the wide curving staircase to the landing, where she paused and looked
down, her heart beating as loudly as if she had
been chased. And he was standing there, in the
centre of the doorway, legs apart, hands thrust into
the waistband of his slacks, looking up at her, no
longer smiling but with a speculative, disturbing
expression on his dark handsome face.

Victoria turned and fled, as silently as she could
on the bare polished boards, in the direction of her
bedroom. She lay against the closed door, her heart
thundering as if she had the devil himself after her.
The thought came to her mind, at once bringing a
faint smile to her lips. The devil. She levered herself
from the door and walked slowly across to the
window, undoing the catch of her bracelet as she
did so and cradling it in the palm of one hand. She
leaned forward on the sill, trying to catch a
glimpse of the front door but finding it was out of
sight from this position, and even as she looked
the patch of light narrowed and disappeared. She
waited, then heard a bolt being secured, and
silence.

The devil—how often she had used the word as

an apt description of her employer. How often she had thought his surname inappropiate for a man of his temperament. And yet she had read some-where that the Angel Gabriel was sometimes known as the angel of fire and thunder, and that somehow seemed appropriate.

She walked over to the dressing table and sank on to the stool with a sudden realisation of how exhausted she felt. She looked at herself for a moment, admiring the simple lines of the blue lawn dress with its deeply scooped neckline, putting up her hands to unclip the short silver chain round her neck which matched her bracelet. And as she bent her head, in the glass she caught sight of the corner of the large bed draped with its thick white cotton bedspread. Slowly she swung round in her seat and stared at it, filled with an unexpected and unbearable loneliness.

The party was a surprise popped on them by Helen and Janet as they finished a light lunch out on the lawn the following day.

'Oh, by the way, don't plan anything for this evening,' Helen began to collect their plates and pile them on a tray, 'because we've asked one or two friends round later on.' She turned, balancing the tray against one hip.

'Oh?' Benedict looked up at the two older women, his eyes hidden behind dark glasses, one hand reaching into the breast pocket of his shirt for a cigarette which he put between his lips and lit. 'Oh?' he repeated, pulling smoke into his lungs and then waiting.

'That's one thing you must do, Victoria.' There

was a faint colour in Helen's cheeks as she changed the subject. 'You must make him give up smoking—such a bad habit.'

'Oh, he hardly does at all now.' Victoria glanced quickly from her mother-in-law to Benedict. 'He . . .'

'You were speaking of this evening, Mother . . .' His voice was dangerously quiet.

'Now don't be blaming your mother, Ben.' Janet got up and firmly took the tray from her employer. 'If anyone's to blame it's me. She told me that you'd forbidden her to do anything like that, but I didn't think it was right. What would people think? What would your wife think?' And with that she led the way towards the house, Helen following after an apologetic glance in Victoria's direction, leaving her son staring out to sea, a very black expression on his face.

'Do I gather,' Victoria spoke only when it became obvious that he had no intention of breaking the silence, 'that you'd expressly forbidden them to have guests in while we were here?'

'I had. If there's one thing I can't stand it's these affairs where people stand about wittering with drinks and damp pieces of toast in their hands.'

'Is that your only objection?' she asked coldly. 'Or do you simply want to make it clear to all and sundry that our wedding is something you don't feel like celebrating?'

'Well, that too, of course.' Benedict got up from his chair and stood looking down at her, one hand pressed against his back in a way that she guessed

was meant to remind her that he had spent an un-
comfortable night on a sofa in the summerhouse.
'But mainly what I told you. If there's one thing I
hate it's the average drinks party.'

Victoria felt the colour leave her face and she
stood up to face him. 'You really are the most in-
sufferably rude brute I've ever met!' She shook
back some hair that had fallen over her face. 'Does
it ever occur to you that some day you might meet
someone who'll be able to hurt you as much
as . . .'

To her surprise he laughed and his expression
changed. 'Of course it has, my darling. And I
apologise.' He caught her hand in his and raised it
to his lips. 'And to you too, Mother.' As he spoke
over her shoulder Victoria heard the rattle of cups
behind her. 'I've no right to do the three most
important females in my life out of a small celebration. I'll try to be the perfect son—and the perfect husband.' Behind the glasses his eyes taunted
Victoria.

'Oh, good.' Helen turned to Janet, who was following with a pot of steaming coffee in her hand.
'Well, that's a relief. You'd made such a point of
neither of you wanting a fuss that we'd become
quite nervous, hadn't we, Janet?'

'Yes—at least you had. But why you can't do
what you want in your own house I don't know.
You've always had too much of your own way,'
Janet nodded her head severely in Benedict's direction. 'I hope you won't be like that with your own
sons.'

'No, I'm determined not to be, Janet.' He seemed
not the least bit put out by her remonstrance. 'My

children will be perfect in every way. Not a bit like their father.'

'Well, then we'll have Victoria to thank for that, not you. Now both of you sit down and have this coffee before it gets cold.'

'Oh, and maybe you should both go and lie down this afternoon,' Helen put in. 'It's so hot and . . .'

'Oh, I don't think I will . . .' Victoria spoke quickly. 'I don't feel the least bit tired, I told you I slept like a log last night. But maybe Benedict would.' She smiled sweetly at him across the table. 'Would you, darling? I think you said you were feeling a bit sleepy. And that bed is so soft and comfortable . . .'

'Yes, I might at that.' His eyes taunted her. 'I have a bit of sleep to make up.' He paused significantly. 'After last night.'

And as she felt the colour flood into her face Victoria glared at him as if she would have liked to kill him.

After lunch she slipped upstairs and changed into her bikini, pulling a short towelling jacket on top before she quickly ran down again and out across the grass on to the beach. It was a glorious day, the sun shining down from an almost cloudless sky and only the faintest breeze coming off the sea. She wandered along the sand, past the cottages scattered along the tiny bay, enjoying the way the hot sand squeezed between her bare toes.

Then she turned and made her way back towards the gate of Trezance and lying down in the sun she pulled a paperback book from her pocket and began to read. But within a few minutes she drifted off to sleep and woke with a start later feeling over-warm and sticky, longing for a swim. She threw off her jacket and walked down to the shore, plunging into the cold water, enjoying the delicious coolness on her hot skin.

When she felt refreshed she climbed back up the beach, squeezing her hair out and feeling the water running down her neck. Then she picked up her jacket from the sand, pulled it round her shoulders and ran lightly towards the house.

She was in the bathroom, about to push the plug into the deep old-fashioned bath and turn on the polished brass tap, when she remembered that her hair drier was in the bedroom next door. She imagined that Benedict was still there, sleeping off the discomfort of the previous night in the deep double bed. She tiptoed along to the firmly closed door, tapped very softly and when there was no response opened it very gently and without looking at the bed she walked softly on her bare feet across to the dressing table.

The drawer opened soundlessly, her fingers were closing over the drier when she heard him turn over in the bed, and when she looked quickly into the mirror, the yellow eyes were studying her impassively.

'I'm sorry.' She was breathless. 'I hope I didn't wake you. I just came for this.' She turned round, holding up the drier ostentatiously.

'No, you didn't wake me. I'd been coming to the surface for some time. I didn't even hear you come in. I simply turned and there you were.' With a sudden move he threw back the covers, pulling himself up to a sitting position, then running a hand through his dishevelled dark hair.

'Oh!' Victoria felt she was rooted to the spot, and the sight of that expanse of brown skin liberally strewn with hair was doing curious things to her insides.

'Would you throw over a cigarette.' He was looking at her as if only too well aware of the effect he was having on her. 'In my shirt pocket on the chair.'

'Yes, of course.' She put down the hair drier and walked across to where she could see his shirt carelessly tossed down with his other things, pulled out the pack of cigarettes and took them over to the bed.

'Thanks.' Languidly he took out a cigarette and put it between his lips. 'You'll have to wait to begin your conversion, I'm afraid.' One eyebrow was raised questioningly. 'Am I to have a light?'

Without speaking Victoria went back to his shirt and brought out the slim lighter, handing it to him without comment.

'Thanks.' The light flared and he narrowed his eyes against the smoke. 'Sit down, Victoria.' He patted the bed beside him in a disarming way. 'It's a bed for two, after all.'

'No, thanks.' Nervously she took a step backwards, for the first time remembering that she was wearing a very scanty bikini. 'My costume will still be wet.'

'It looks dry to me. And your hair's beginning to curl, did you know.' He blew the smoke in a narrow stream away from her. 'Go on, sit down. You look like Red Riding Hood about to be eaten by the wolf.'

'What did you mean about conversion?' Quickly she changed the subject.

'Your instructions from my mother that I'm to give up smoking. If you can do that you'll make your mark even more than you have done already.'

'But you'd almost stopped. You seem to be slipping back. I thought you had more self-control.'

'I have more self-control than you'll ever know.' His voice was tight and hard now. 'And if you stand there any longer you might find that it's slipped.'

Without answering Victoria whirled away from him and almost ran to the door. She paused with the knob in her hand, fighting the panic that she was afraid he might have recognised. 'Will you be long? I'd like to change when I come out of the bath.'

'You won't worry me.' He smiled at her disarmingly.

'Oh . . .' Angrily she began to close the door.

'Victoria!' His voice was imperative, staying her impulsive action.

'Yes?' She paused by the almost closed door, refusing to look towards him.

'Don't forget your hair drier.'

She pushed the door open, strode across to the dressing-table and as she banged the door closed she heard him laughing very softly to himself.

But by the time they assembled for the party they had resumed their pose as happy newlyweds. Victoria had chosen the dress she had worn on the night when they had been married, when Benedict had taken her out to dinner. It was extravagantly admired when they came downstairs together and obediently she turned once or twice so that Helen and Janet would be denied nothing of the effect.

'Yes, completely charming, Victoria. And it's not the kind of dress that everyone can wear. It takes style to carry it off.'

'Yes,' Janet was ready to add her warm approval, 'you need a figure with a dress like that. I've no patience with these young women nowadays. Some of the ones Benedict's brought home . . .' She shook her head disapprovingly.

'I'm inclined to agree with you, Janet.' Benedict put his arm round his wife, pulled her towards him and smiled down at her. 'Victoria knows what I think of her in this dress, don't you, my sweet?'

'Of course I do, darling.' She put up a hand and stroked his smooth freshly shaved cheek. 'I know.' She lowered her voice intimately and fluttered her eyelashes.

'Quite an actress, aren't you?' He moved away as quickly as he could when Helen and Janet left them to go into the kitchen to put some finishing touches to the food they had prepared.

'I'm doing my best to follow your example.' Her smile was sweet as she turned to follow them. 'Darling!' she finished in cloying tones as she pushed open the kitchen door and took refuge with her mother-in-law.

The party had been in progress for more than an hour and Victoria was talking to James and Patricia Jenkins from two doors away up the lane when she heard a shout from the direction of the door leading from the drawing-room into the hall. When she turned round, she saw standing there one of the largest, in every way, men she had ever seen in her life. He was built like an ancient oak, solid, thick and heavy, and on top of his huge torso, his head was covered with dark curling hair and his face with a matching beard. At the moment it was split in a wide grin, showing white teeth, and he reminded Victoria of one of those puzzles which used to figure in children's pages in newspapers—turn him upside down to see his brother. His voice was as big as the rest of him and as he called out Benedict's name the room grew quiet while everyone turned round towards the source of the commotion.

'Oh, it's Brian,' Patricia explained with a smile. 'When those two get together! I wonder ...' She looked towards the door again, 'has he brought Sam with him? Isn't she ...? Oh yes, there she is.' And following the direction of her gaze Victoria saw a blonde young woman dressed in a loose Indian muslin dress and very obviously pregnant follow Brian into the room. 'You'd better go, Victoria. Ben is looking round for you. He'll want to introduce you to his best friend.'

'Pity the third musketeer isn't here tonight,' James put in, 'but I think Dave is still abroad.'

'Would you excuse me?' Victoria had caught Benedict's eye as he turned round, his arm round his friend's shoulder, his head turned to speak down to the small girl on his other side.

'Yes, of course. And next time we'll tell you about some of the tricks they got up to when they were kids. Ask Ben about the buried treasure.'

'So this is Victoria.' She found her hand completely enveloped in a huge paw while bright keen blue eyes tried to bore through hers. 'Well, I'd say she was worth waiting for. What do you think, Sam?' he asked his wife.

The girl merely smiled sympathetically at Victoria, apparently realising that her husband wouldn't wait for an answer.

'Yes, you old devil!' He gave Benedict a playful thump on the chest. 'You know, lovey,' he spoke with the soft local burr which Victoria found enchanting, 'we made solemn promises to each other— he was to be my best man and I was to be his. Then he springs this terrible surprise on us, does us out of all the shindig.'

'I'm sorry, it was a bit sudden. I . . .' Victoria apologised.

'Oh well, I'm not the sort to bear a grudge. And to tell the truth I might not have been able to make it up to London just at the moment.' He reached out and put an arm round his wife, pulling her affectionately against him. 'We might not have felt like travelling with Sam in her delicate condition.' His wife smiled up at him as if she was used to his teasing and didn't mind. 'She's promised me a son finally haven't you, love?' he squeezed her shoulders.

'You're sure this time, are you?' It was the first time anyone else had had the chance to speak. 'I seem to have heard that before,' Benedict grinned down at Sam.

'Oh, she knows the score at last, Ben. If it's another disappointment I'm ready to do a Henry the Eighth. There's that buxom barmaid in the Dog and Gun—name's Anne.'

'Have you a girl already?' Victoria determined

to break into what she was afraid could easily develop into a monologue.

'Three.' Sam smiled faintly. 'Last time we thought third time lucky. But this is my last attempt. If . . .'

'If it's another girl, then we'll try again. What do you say, Ben, doesn't every man long to have a son?'

'Shut up, darling.' Sam noticed the colour in Victoria's cheeks and at last asserted herself with a firmness which Victoria found at once surprising and refreshing. 'You do love to act the male chauvinist. Do you think you're convincing Ben?'

'Why . . .?' Brian pulled down the corners of his mouth and held his hands up appealingly. 'Tell me why I should trouble to convince Ben? It's you I'd like to convince, my love.' He turned to Victoria and slipped a hand through her arm. 'Come on, Victoria, let's leave the pair of them together for a while. There's a lot I can tell you about the man you've married!'

And for the rest of the evening Victoria found that Brian was her companion, content apparently to pour into her listening ear all the reminiscences that presumably the rest of the guests had heard previously. When supper was served Benedict did come and claim her, standing with his arm about her waist while James Jenkins spoke a few words of congratulations, and then with every appearance of sincerity responding in a short amusing speech during which he allowed himself to look at her fondly, his eyes to linger on her face, finally raising his bubbling glass to her.

'To my wife.'

'To Benedict.' Although her words were sweetly spoken, her manner wifely, her eyes mocked him and she was pleased when he turned from her with well-concealed annoyance.

The rest of the weekend slipped by quickly with apparently no one realising that the summerhouse was used by an overnight guest. There was one awkward moment when Helen was walking round the garden with Benedict and Victoria, when they stopped by the hut and Helen peered through the glass.

'Why, there's a towel inside. I can't . . .'

'Oh, that was me, Mother,' Benedict interrupted smoothly. 'I was awake early this morning and couldn't get back to sleep, so I crept downstairs. I didn't want to wake Victoria, she looked so peaceful, so I came down, through the back door and I locked it behind me—you needn't think I left the house wide open for vandals and vagrants. I swam across the bay just as the sun was coming up. And when I came back I changed in the summerhouse, then I lay reading a book for an hour or two.'

'Ah, I see. I ought to have had it opened up, I suppose. I just forgot. Janet and I don't often go in when we're alone. A pity . . .' She spoke with a tinge of sadness. 'The old house isn't used as much as it ought to be. I don't suppose . . .' she hesitated, '. . . there's no chance that you and Victoria might come down here to live? Janet and I have been thinking of moving somewhere smaller.'

'I don't think so, Mother.' There was a faint harshness about Benedict's response. 'We have quite a commitment to London, you know. It's best to be near the centre of things. And possibly

Victoria wouldn't like to live in the country.'

'What do you feel, Victoria?' Helen wrinkled her nose at her son. 'Don't let him have it all his own way. There *is* something in what Janet says about him being spoiled. Would you hate it down here, my dear?'

'Hate it?' Victoria turned and looked over the garden, towards the curve of high copper beeches which gave them complete privacy from the next property, beyond the brightly pink clumps of thrift which nestled in the shelter of the wall and out across the bay where one or two sails drifted lazily into her vision. 'If it were mine I should never want to leave it. It's very nearly my idea of perfection.'

'There!' Helen turned triumphantly to her son. 'I had the feeling that Victoria was a country girl. In that case, we'll hang on for a few years. And you,' she slipped her hand through Victoria's arm, 'do your best to persuade him. If anyone can make him change his mind you can, my dear. And it's such an ideal family house it would be a pity to sell it now. Just when Benedict has married.' She sighed contentedly. 'Now I'm going to help Janet with those sandwiches.' As she left she was singing happily beneath her breath and there was silence for a moment.

'Do you think that was a sensible thing to do?' Benedict's words cut Victoria like a whiplash.

'What was I to do?' she flared back. 'Tell your mother that I didn't care for her house? Tell her a deliberate lie?'

'It's a bit late to worry about lies.'

Victoria stared at him for a long time through narrowed eyes. 'Yes,' she said at last. 'But try to remember just whose idea that was.'

'Yes, it was mine—I confess it.' He shrugged his shoulders, unexpectedly amused. 'I walked into it with my eyes wide open. But it still puzzles me why you agreed to such a preposterous suggestion, Miss Kendall. I find it a very intriguing problem, one that I would give anything to solve.'

Victoria felt a stab of pain as he spoke. A preposterous suggestion? They had been married less than three weeks and already he was referring to their situation in those terms. And Miss Kendall! She felt a sob rise in her throat, tears sting behind her eyes making them glitter with what might have been anger.

'Hasn't it occurred to you, Mr Gabriell,' she tried to match her own cool mockery to his, 'hasn't it occurred to you that perhaps it was too good an opportunity to miss? The chance to pay back all those insults, all those times when it was "cancel your date, Miss Kendall, I want you to retype this letter", all those bouts of moody bad temper.' She laughed. 'You made me a very tempting offer, Mr Gabriell, one that when I'd recovered from the initial incredulity I found I could scarcely refuse.'

'You little . . .' He took a step towards her, gripping her arms fiercely in strong cruel fingers. 'Are you telling me that you planned this simply to make life difficult for me?'

'Of course.' She laughed. 'You didn't think it was because you'd made yourself irresistible, did you? If you believe that you must be very naïve indeed, Mr Gabriell.'

Abruptly he dropped his hands, an expression of disgust curling his mouth. 'At this moment I could believe almost anything of you.' The flecks of brown in his eyes seemed to make them flame with anger.

Without another word Victoria turned on her heel and walked swiftly towards the house. Only by the exercise of the greatest self-control did she prevent herself from rushing across the grass with tears streaming down her cheeks.

CHAPTER FIVE

THEIR journey back to London was completed in an atmosphere of stilted politeness which was a relief after the false affection which Victoria had felt obliged to keep up for the sake of Helen and Janet. Once or twice she noticed that Benedict's conspicuously cool manner had provoked a few reproving glances from Janet.

'Don't be upset by him,' she advised Victoria when later they were washing up in the kitchen. 'He'd most likely got his mind on one of his books or some such. He's best just left alone till he comes round. He's always been the same. When he has something to think about the rest of us needn't exist.'

Victoria polished the plate she was drying with excessive thoroughness. 'Don't worry, Janet. I haven't been his secretary for all these years without getting to know him pretty well.'

'That's good.' Janet smiled her relief. 'You know,' she looked a bit shamefaced as she made the confession, 'although I put him in his place from time to time I'm as fond of him as if he were my own. You see, I brought him up really. His mother was so ill, losing her husband so early, that when he was born she couldn't care for him herself and I was asked to come for six months. Well,' her smile illuminated her plain face, 'here I am still, goodness knows how many years later.

I've always been treated like one of the family and they *are* my family now. I can't tell you what a relief it was to us, his mother and me, when we met you. You'll be good for him. He needs someone who'll make a home for him, give him children. Not that there's any hurry for that,' she added with judicious tact. 'No, now that he's found the right girl our minds are at rest.'

But Janet's mind wouldn't have been at rest if she had been able to eavesdrop, to perch invisibly on the back of their seats during the drive. She would have been shocked—and as frightened as Victoria was herself at the abrupt change from the charm Benedict had exerted on the way down to Cornwall.

It was a relief when he suggested going up to the office before they returned to Peverell Square, and Victoria's enthusiasm had a tinge of hysteria in it.

'Right.' He swung the car out of the mainstream of traffic and headed towards the mews where his office was situated. 'We'll just go up and see what mail has come in. We needn't wait, I know you'll be tired.' As they stopped at a red light he glanced in her direction with the first sign of consideration he had shown.

'No, I'm not tired.' Firmly avoiding his eyes, Victoria stared away from them towards the late afternoon shoppers walking along the tree-lined street, her vision distorted by the gush of tears in her eyes.

She fancied a faint sigh from his direction, heard the impatient drum of his fingers on the driving column and the next thing she knew they were drawing up at the familiar polished oak door that led to his upstairs office.

They had finished dealing with the mail, none of which was unduly important, and were about to bang the door behind them when the telephone rang.

'I'll get it.' Victoria was across the room in a moment, glad of any excuse which would delay their return home for even a few moments longer. 'It's for you.' She handed him the scarlet receiver. 'Jeremy Ransome.' She sat down at her desk, listening with only half an ear, aware of the vague murmur of the voice at the other end, the terse, slightly impatient replies from Benedict. But suddenly he put his hand over the mouthpiece, swinging round to look at her as she leafed through the latest copy of *Vogue*.

'It's Jeremy,' he told her unnecessarily. 'He's having some sort of party tonight, some Americans are here to discuss the possibility of making a programme on one of the islands in the Gilbert group and he wants me to be there. I've said no, but perhaps you feel you would like to go.'

'No.' Without raising her eyes to look at him she continued her aimless search of the pages. 'No, thank you. But don't refuse on my account. I shall be very happy to go to bed when I've had something to eat. As you told me,' she paused before putting the magazine down with a sigh and looking up at him, 'I'm tired.'

The golden eyes blazed down at her in a quick unexpected flare of anger. 'Is that what you want?' His voice was as cold as his glance was scorching.

She gave a dismissive little smile and shrugged. 'You must do what you want. I've told you, I want to go and sleep.' Unable to withstand the contemptuous anger she saw on his face, she got up and strolled towards the door. 'I should go.' Her voice was a shade more conciliatory now. 'They're *your* friends, after all. And it seems as if they might be the kind of people you should meet.'

'Jeremy,' without taking his eyes from her Benedict removed his hand from the telephone, 'that's all right.' Abruptly he turned his back so that Victoria was left looking at the way his hair grew thick and waving at the back of his neck, at the broad shoulders under the lightweight tweed jacket. 'No, I'll be alone.' His tone was lighter now, more amused, as if the prospect of an evening on his own with friends was one that was all at once appealing. Straining to hear now, Victoria was thwarted by the low murmur and the burst of amusement that came over the line. But then Benedict's slow deep laugh brought the colour to her face. 'No, nothing like that.' And she knew that somehow a joke had been made at her expense.

It wasn't long before she was regretting her cavalier, almost rude rejection of his invitation. From the moment when he had come to the door of her bedroom, knocking lightly and not opening the door until she called to him, she had had the feeling of being left out of things. Perhaps the sight of him in a velvet jacket in a dark plum shade, the dazzling white of his shirt making her long to reach out and touch his darkly tanned skin, perhaps that made her realise how dangerous it could be to choose to let him go to a party on his own. And in the pecu-

liar mood which was affecting them both. She had
a sudden almost overwhelming longing to tell him
to wait, to give her time to go and throw on the
short evening dress which he hadn't yet seen, a
dream of a dress that could make the most unattractive woman look beautiful and desirable. If
he had given the slightest sign! If he had even
asked, Are you sure you won't change your mind?
If he had done that she would have flown to get
ready, her heart singing.

But he didn't. He merely said that he was going
and that she should settle down and have a good
rest. Then he had brushed her cheek with his lips—
near enough for her to smell his cologne, but so
distant that her pride would not let her even hint
that she was regretting her original decision.
Instead she hoped he would enjoy himself, as an
afterthought telling him she was glad she didn't
have to go out again, although the sound of his
whistling as he ran downstairs brought the familiar
crushing pain to her chest. And she ran across to
the window where she could stand, just out of sight
behind the net curtains, watching while he walked
down the garden towards the garage. He paused
once, stooping to pluck a pure white Pascali rose
which he put in the buttonhole of his lapel before
continuing along the path with a spring in his step
that Victoria was convinced was all to do with her
absence.

She had no idea when he came home. No idea
except that it was late, hideously late, later than
three in the morning. That was the time when she
had wakened from a faint doze, shaken from her
drowse by the sudden hammering of her own heart

reminding her of the anxiety besetting her. And she had risen from her bed, and without stopping to pull her dressing gown about her had padded out into the corridor, the carpet soft and warm against her bare feet.

The door of Benedict's bedroom was slightly open, the moonlight spilling across making a streak of white on the floor. Victoria was trembling as she leaned with one hand, gently, making it swing back noiselessly. But the narrow bed was smooth and intact, offering her no relief from her anxious thoughts.

Next time she woke the sun was shining brightly between the gaps where her curtains had not quite met and almost at once the familiar sound of bathwater running in the room next to hers told her that he was back. She had no idea when he returned and she was too proud to ask directly.

'How did it go last night?' Idly she pushed her mother's letter back into its envelope, raising her eyes to look at him across the table.

'Last night?' Abstractedly Benedict glanced up from his newspaper. 'Oh, long-winded, but quite enjoyable. You know how these things are.'

'Mmm.' She didn't remind him that he had never taken her to one. With a casual air she looked away from him, out over the garden. 'Were you very late?'

'Yes, a bit, I suppose.' With an air of great concern he put down his paper and looked at her. 'I hope I didn't disturb you. I tried not to make a sound.'

'No, I didn't hear you come in.' As she spoke she turned towards him, deliberately scrutinising his face for some sign of relief. She thought she discerned it, but could not be certain.

It was later that same morning that two things happened, sufficiently unusual for Victoria to wonder afterwards at the coincidence. She was in the midst of typing some of the notes Benedict had asked her to prepare for his television show at the end of the week when the telephone rang and, pre-occupied, she picked it up.

'Hello. Guess who?'

'I'm sorry,' she answered crisply, irritated that the caller was so coy about giving his name, 'I'm busy and . . .'

'Come on, love!' the laughing voice invited. 'It's bad enough to come home and find my favourite date is married, then to be told she's forgotten the very sound of my voice . . .'

'Iain!' In spite of herself there was no concealing the pleasure the thought of him brought. 'Iain, how absolutely wonderful! I thought you were in New Guinea.'

'I was until a few days ago. I thought that was the arrangement. Three years out there and then you'd give me the answer to my question. I . . .'

But at that very moment Victoria heard a tiny, almost inaudible little sound that brought her head round quickly towards the door leading towards the inner office. Was it possible that Benedict had picked up the telephone in his office just a split second before she had lifted the receiver? It wasn't something he did often, but could he by chance have heard what was really a very personal con-versation? And did he consider it so personal that he didn't want Victoria to know that he had over-heard? With an effort she dragged her mind back to what was being said.

'. . . And that's why I rang. I'm going back to Harrogate at the weekend and wondered if there was a chance of you escaping long enough to have a meal with me?'

'Oh, Iain, I'm sorry. I'm going to be so busy for the next few days preparing for the programme and . . .'

'That's right, rub it in! Remind me that I can't compete with the glamorous world of the television personalities. I should have insisted on taking you with me three years ago and . . .'

'Oh, Iain, I'm sorry—I must go.' Victoria spun round in her seat as the door opened, as if by con-cealing the telephone she would hide from Benedict that she was speaking to someone. Behind her she heard him walk to the filing cabinet and begin to riffle through files, another unusual action. An impatient sigh came towards her.

'Well, can I give you my telephone number, sweetie?' For the first time she realised just how loud a voice Iain had. 'I would like to see you, have a drink, even if you can't spare time for a meal.'

'Oh, all right.' She knew this was the quickest way of getting rid of him and quickly jotted down the number he read out to her.

'And you will try, Victoria?'

'Yes, truly I'll try. Goodbye.' She put down the receiver and turned to watch Benedict's apparently fruitless search in the top drawer. 'Can I help you?' She hated the way his impatience was disturbing the perfection of her filing system.

'I hope so. If you've finished your private conversation.' His eyebrows were drawn together in an angry frown.

'Yes, I have finished.' Coolly she got up and walked towards him, seeing how his gaze lingered with ill-concealed irritation on the crisp navy and white cotton dress she was wearing. Without saying any more she took the manilla folder from him, looked at its heading and slipped it into its proper position. Then she looked at him, her lips firm, her eyes cold. 'Well?' She asked at last.

'It's that data on my 1975 trip to Kasos. I thought of something that might be relevant, a reference I might be able to use on the show on Friday.'

'It won't be in this drawer.' It gave her considerable satisfaction to be able to close the compartment with a firm hand. 'You remember you asked me some time ago to cross-reference those trips by dates instead of title. It'll be in the bottom . . .' She knelt down and began methodically with slender pink-tipped fingers to search for the right date. Then once again she looked through before sitting back on her heels, a puzzled frown on her features. 'That's strange.' She put her fingers to her forehead, then looked up at him. 'But isn't that the file you took home last week? You said something about one of the other islands. That you'd like to bring up to date the guide you published . . .'

'Damn!' Benedict thumped himself on the forehead with a clenched fist. 'Damn!' He strode back into his office, banging the door behind him, leaving Victoria in a mood of smouldering anger.

If she had thought, she told herself as she hammered away at her machine, if she had imagined that he would not treat his wife as badly as he had treated his secretary she had been foolishly optimistic. In fact she had quite simply been a fool. She pounded at the keys, ignoring the sound of the door opening behind her, pretending she was unaware that his figure lounging in the doorway was reflected in the large pane of glass in the door leading out on to the landing. But she could not pretend that her body was unaware of him, for the very suspicion he was purposefully about to exert his persuasions was enough to bring a throb of anticipation to her quivering senses.

'Victoria.' When she was forced to pause to change a sheet of paper he came forward to perch on the edge of her desk.

'Yes?' She frowned in concentration as if the simple task demanded it, then leaned over her notebook, hands poised above the keys.

'Victoria.' He reached out with a deep laugh and picked up the book, causing her eyes to fly open in indignation.

'I'm busy!' she flared. 'You said you must have that draft by teatime and . . .'

'Don't get angry. I . . .'

'Don't get angry!' she repeated with controlled sarcasm. 'You are the last person on earth to give such advice to . . .'

'I know, I know.' The gold eyes gleamed down at her in amusement. 'I'm a brute to work for. But now I must have those notes about Kasos, Victoria. And I just can't leave the office. You know I'm expecting that call from Paramond in the States.

And you,' he pulled a bunch of keys from his pocket and dangled them in front of her, 'you could be home in twenty minutes and back here in less than an hour.'

'You—you would let me drive your car?' she wavered, unable to resist the flattering suggestion.

'Our car, Victoria. Our car. That's what being married means, after all. And I'm not sure that I find your astonishment very encouraging. In fact I have as much confidence in your driving as in most of your other qualities. Oh, and,' he dropped the keys on her desk and turned away as if the entire matter had been resolved to their mutual satisfaction, 'I did tell you that I have to go out for lunch today. So if . . .'

'No.' Victoria paused in the act of picking up the keys. 'No, you didn't tell me.'

'Oh, didn't I?' Benedict turned round from the door of his inner sanctum. 'I thought I had. So what I was going to say, my sweet, is, don't rush back.'

'No?' Her query was sardonic. 'Thanks. And you won't want this draft by teatime after all.'

He shrugged and grinned at her, that calculatingly frank smile which in spite of all her experience made her own lips long to curve into a response. 'As I've told you often enough in the past, Victoria, my bark is worse than my bite.'

'I don't remember.' She turned away to hide the softening of her expression, then paused with her hand on the door knob. 'Oh, won't you want your car for your lunch date?' She swung round unexpectedly, her dark eyebrows raised enquiringly.

'Oh . . .' For a split second he looked almost

taken aback. 'No, I can always ring for a taxi at a push. Thanks, love.' Then he turned away with every appearance of anxiety to return to work and Victoria went downstairs slowly, trying to resolve a faint niggling query at the back of her mind.

Of course, she thought as she edged carefully into the stream of traffic at the roundabout, he had been very cagey about his luncheon appointment. Usually he told her where he would be so that she could contact him if necessary. Then she remembered. He had said that he couldn't leave the office because of the call he was expecting from Paramond. Then a moment later that she needn't rush back. It was almost as if he were feeling guilty about something and was getting his lines crossed—usually when he was going out for some kind of business lunch he liked to have her in the office. Anyway, she shrugged her shoulders as she changed into low gear to take the sharp corner into Peverell Square, there was no sense in trying to understand the man. And she needn't think that just because she was now his wife suddenly, magically, the complexities of his inner self would be revealed.

The door with the polished lion's mask swung open soundlessly as she turned her key in the lock. 'It's me, Lumsden,' she called vaguely in the direction of the kitchen, but hearing no answer she turned swiftly and without pausing began to run up the flight of shallow curving steps, her feet moving soundlessly on the thickly carpeted treads.

There was a sense of something strange, unexpected which was too vague for her to identify until she reached the upper landing, where she paused, her hand dropping from the balustrade, a puzzled little frown between her eyebrows. It was a scent, exotic yet faintly astringent, distinctive enough, although Victoria had met only once the woman who claimed it had been designed especially for her. Perhaps knowing the woman made Victoria dislike the fragrance, imagine that it stung the back of the throat, was altogether too positive, too overwhelming. Rather like the Baroness herself, in fact.

Even as the association led her mind inexorably to the name which had been so closely associated with her husband, from the open door of Benedict's bedroom she heard the murmur of voices; the deeper tones were easily enough identified as Lumsden's, but the light answering gurgle of laughter could only belong to one woman. Her heart was hammering as she took a few uncertain steps forward, as if she and not this other woman was the intruder. Then there was a further soft interchange from the hidden couple, a shadow moved across the open door and Baroness Kertesz stepped into the hallway.

For once she appeared slightly taken aback, but recovered swiftly.

'Oh, I did not hear anyone,' she said calmly.

'Obviously.' Victoria felt patches of colour in her cheeks, but refused to be further intimidated by the expression on the other woman's face. She looked at Lumsden, who had appeared suddenly behind the Baroness, looking rather foolish for once, the cloth in his hand as well as the sound of running water indicating that he had been cleaning the bath. As she continued to wait for an explanation, he seemed to gather his wits.

'The Baroness, madam,' now there was a vestige
of a smile on his face, a slightly self-satisfied smile,
'has come round to collect something she left here
on a,' he coughed in mock apology, 'on a previous
occasion.'

'Yes.' The Baroness spoke and as she did so,
held up her clenched fist, then opened it with an
air of a conjuror producing the rabbit, 'this.' A
slim jewelled lipstick case lay on her pale elegant
palm. 'It was a present from my husband and
rather precious. And last night when I asked Ben
if . . .'

'You saw Benedict last night?' The words were
regretted as soon as spoken.

'Yes.' There was a faint gurgle of amusement
and Victoria could not miss the understanding look
that passed between Lumsden, who had come forward into the hall, and the Baroness. But he
showed no emotion as he turned towards his employer.

'You came home to collect something, madam?'

'Yes. Some papers for my husband.' She brushed
past him into Benedict's bedroom. 'He left them
here a night or two ago.'

'If you would tell me where they were left,
madam, perhaps I could help you.' Lumsden had
followed her into the room and Victoria could see
without looking round the tall figure of the woman
lounging in the doorway.

'That won't be necessary, Lumsden, thank you.'
She knelt down by the bedside table and began to
leaf quickly through some papers on the lower
shelf.

'I was going to make some coffee for the Baroness.' Again there was the suggestion of a swift interchange of glances. 'Perhaps you would care for a cup too, madam.'

'No, I don't think so, thank you, Lumsden. Ah!' Swiftly Victoria extracted the folder she was looking for. 'Here it is.' She stood up. 'Well, perhaps I might take time after all.' Her smile included them both. 'That is, if the Baroness would care to join me?' She found a faint pleasure in emphasising just who had the right to invite guests for coffee.

'Very well, madam.' Lumsden inclined his head and a moment later he had left them, without waiting for the Baroness's reaction, which he appeared able to take for granted.

There was a long silence while the two women took stock of each other, but it took Victoria only an instant to remember the pangs of burning jealousy that their only previous meeting had evoked. Then she had appeared in the office one day just before lunch, immaculately perfect for her date with Benedict. And Victoria, who had had a particularly frantic morning without a moment to powder her nose or tidy her hair, had felt sweaty and untidy and at a considerable disadvantage. She had also resented the disdainful amusement on the beautiful face when they had been introduced.

'Oh, your typist, Ben darling. How do you do, Miss Kendall.'

'But you mustn't call her that, Camilla.' His eyes had glinted at Victoria, noticing her dishevelled annoyance and mocking her. 'She's much more to me than that. She's my right hand. She even corrects my spelling sometimes.' With those few words he seemed to have put her firmly into the middle-aged spinster category and Victoria had glared at him.

'Oh.' Camilla had shuddered delicately under her red fox jacket. 'Spelling!' And she had moved away as if her immaculate black harem trousers might get some dust from Victoria's table. 'I think you're wonderful to do it.' She hadn't found it necessary to explain exactly what she meant, but the implication was clear enough. Boring old nine-to-five jobs were not for the likes of her.

When they had left Victoria had hammered savagely at her typewriter in an unusual fury, refusing even to stop to snatch the sandwiches she had brought with her that day. She wouldn't have minded so much if Camilla Kertesz was anybody. Really anybody. She was only a baroness at all because some third-rate baron from some semi-extinct state had seen her picture in a glossy magazine and had lifted her out of the world of fashion photography before he had killed himself in a car crash. Although if her clothes were anything to go by, he had left her fairly well provided for.

Even today, standing in the middle of Benedict's bedroom glaring at her, one could not deny that the Baroness had style. So much so that Victoria felt clumsy, gauche and the navy and white dress which had pleased her so much when she put it on this morning was now—not dowdy exactly, but just not smart. And Camilla's swift dismissive glance merely confirmed her own opinion.

But Camilla was elegant, simply elegant in a black cotton shift that skimmed over her slim body, scarcely touching those narrow boy's hips. Several long ropes of pearls reached almost to her waist and in the small ears matching stones gleamed. Her face was long and narrow, made longer by the way she chose to wear her long black hair braided and piled into a coronet on the top of her head. This also exaggerated her height, which was intimidating at any time, for she and Benedict were almost equally matched, as more than one gossip columnist had mentioned.

'The long leggy Baroness Kertesz, who is the constant companion of one of our best known television interviewers.' 'Not perhaps the most beautiful but without argument the tallest and certainly the most fascinating.' And under the picture of the Baroness modelling beachwear in Bali, 'Who says you need curves to be sensational in a bikini?'

And Victoria, hopelessly gazing at the long limbs contorting on the pale sand, at the languorous fingers pretending to brush strands of silky hair from lips that pouted towards the camera, could not disagree. It was hopeless to try to understand why, but the Baroness *was* sensational in a bikini. So why should she even imagine that Benedict had looked at her in any special way that afternoon in the bedroom in Cornwall when she was so entirely different?

A wave of fresh colour struck her cheeks and she returned to the present with a guilty jump to find a speculative look in the other woman's dark eyes. 'I ... I just want to go to my room to get something.'

'Oh yes. To your room.' The tone in the Baroness's voice told Victoria that their situation had been discussed.

'So if you care to go down to the sitting-room, I'll meet you there.' Her voice was cold. 'I presume you know the way.'

'Oh yes, perfectly.' And with an amused look, Camilla Kertesz turned and walked easily towards the top of the stair, and even the back of her head appeared to convey a sense of amusement that Victoria should imagine herself to be the woman in Benedict Gabriell's life.

'And now,' with an air of assurance she was far from feeling Victoria got to her feet, reaching out a hand for the folder which had been lying on the sofa beside her, 'you'll have to excuse me, Baroness.' She looked down at the woman who was lying back so relaxed in the deep comfortable chair that she might have had no intention of moving. 'I have to get back. So,' in spite of her intention to remain cool she felt the colour in her cheeks again, 'if you'd just like me to show you out . . .'

Baroness Kertesz raised her thin dark eyebrows, removing the need to comment, and with one lithe move she stood towering over Victoria.

'I'm so glad you reminded me,' she purred, glancing at the small diamond-studded watch on her wrist. 'I'd hate to be late for my lunch date with Ben.' The dark eyes mocked Victoria openly. 'Not that he ever minds waiting for me, of course. Goodbye, Miss . . . Mrs Gabriell. I'm so glad to have had the opportunity of meeting Ben's . . . Ben's wife.' She opened the door and swayed across the hall, murmuring a few words to Lumsden who had come hurrying across from the direction of the kitchen just as if he had been waiting behind the door.

But Victoria scarcely was aware of him, even when he came into the sitting-room and began collecting the coffee things on the silver tray. She saw his lips move when he stood to ask her something and was aware of the faint satisfied smile on his face as he turned away from her.

But all she understood at that minute was the pain in her chest as if someone had struck a great blow under her heart. They were having lunch together. Last night at the party she had refused to attend Ben had met Camilla again, and they had arranged to have lunch together today. That was the explanation for his slightly more relaxed attitude towards her. It wasn't that he had forgiven her for the things she had said that last day in Cornwall. It was simply that he was happy because he had met Camilla again.

Oh ... Victoria caught her lips between her teeth, pressing until she felt the warm faintly salty taste of blood on her tongue. But before she had time to consider she found herself reaching out for the telephone, wrinkling her forehead as she tried to recall the number that Iain had given her a short time before. Then she was talking to him, listening with a great easing of her pain as he expressed his pleasure at her change of plans. And when she replaced the receiver she found that most of the tears had dried on her cheeks.

CHAPTER SIX

VICTORIA had no idea why she had chosen to meet Iain at Lalo's. In retrospect it was the last place they should have gone, but at the time, some longing to see the place which she had heard mentioned so often, perhaps even an inclination to assure her companion that she was very much at the centre of things, made her give the name of the place where so many show business personalities took themselves for lunch.

Although that particular day the famous were rather conspicuous by their absence and it crossed Victoria's mind to wonder whether Lalo's day had passed, that those really in the know had found somewhere new to disport themselves. That was until she caught sight of Benedict's dark head leaning towards Camilla's in one of the banquettes. At once she tried to shrink back in her seat and wondered what on earth had possessed her to change into such an eye-catching outfit.

'Did I tell you that you're looking marvellous?' Iain was tall and bronzed from his time in the East, but as dull and matter-of-fact as he had always been.

'Oh, thank you, Iain.' Victoria raised the glass which he had just refilled and raised it to her lips. 'It's a case of fine feathers, I'm afraid.' She smoothed down the knife-pleated skirt of her apricot and black silk suit.

'Nonsense!' he protested stoutly. 'I've always thought so. Even on those days when we used to go out for picnics on the moors at home. You looked just as terrific in jeans and a woollen jumper with your hair flying about your face.' He shrugged. 'In fact, now that I've seen you again I can't understand why I was such a fool. How could I have imagined that a girl like you would still be available when I finally got round to coming home?' He shrugged philosophically. 'I don't blame your boss for sweeping you off your feet.'

'Well, it wasn't quite like that,' honesty made her protest. 'I'd worked with him for a good many years, you know . . .'

'Then obviously *you* couldn't make up your mind, love. Anyway,' he raised his glass in salute, 'I wish you all the luck that's going.' He drank the rich red wine without taking his eyes off her. 'And there's something about the old cliché, you know. Happiness does give a woman a special glow. It's . . .'

'Oh, Iain!' She blushed and looked down at her plate.

'No, I mean it.' He shook his head and looked serious. 'Anyone would notice. I'm just sorry that I wasn't the one to bring that particular look to your eyes. But anyway, you will thank Benedict for sparing you to come with me today.'

You could tell him yourself. As she looked into Iain's frank blue eyes Victoria could see from the preparations that were being made at the table in the far corner that Benedict and his companion were preparing to leave. She saw the waiter present the bill on a plate and a moment later hold Camilla's chair while she rose. Victoria shrank back against the wall and put a hand across her eyes as Benedict turned and glanced vaguely round the room before following Camilla to the door. And as he held the door for her, Camilla stopped, smiling up at him, laying a possessive hand on his jacket. Victoria, who had suspected that Camilla had seen her arrival with Iain, was now sure of it. And she knew that that last little piece of play-acting was for her special benefit.

'Are you listening to me, love?' There was a faintly aggrieved note in Iain's voice which brought her full attention back to him. It cost her an effort to smile, but it was so successful that it appeared to attract the attention of the man who was sitting at the table next to them. In fact he seemed to lose interest in what his male companion was saying, for he turned round in his chair to look at her with interest. Flattered by such an effect, she went so far as to cover Iain's hand with hers for a moment.

'Forgive me, Iain, I thought for a moment that I saw someone I know. What were you saying?'

'I was asking,' it seemed that the touch of her hand was mollifying, for he eagerly turned his round catching her fingers warmly, 'if there was any chance that we might meet before I go back. I'm going up to Yorkshire tomorrow, but I'll be flying back in a month and if we could . . .'

'Oh, but then we might see you in Harrogate.' Feeling that she had shown him more than enough understanding, Victoria withdrew her hand from his and reached for her handbag. 'Benedict and I are going up in about ten days to see Mum and Dad. You know, they haven't even met yet,' a faint colour touched her cheeks, 'and there's a plan that they might be having some sort of party. Naturally your aunt and uncle will be invited and we'd like you to come too. I'll tell Mother when I ring her. And I'd like you to meet Benedict.' Her last words were an afterthought and to her own ears carried little conviction.

It was only later when she was back in the office trying to catch up on the work which her conscience told her she ought to have been doing when she was lunching with Iain that she remembered the file, and realised that she had left it at home after all. Which made it rather fortuitous that Benedict hadn't come back from his lunch engagement.

At least, so she told herself when she tried to damp down the burning pangs of jealousy which assailed her. Only the constant pounding at her typewriter, the careful attention to the pages of shorthand notes kept her fertile thoughts from imagining too closely what Benedict might at this very moment be . . . The shrilling of the telephone brought her sharply back to here and now, and the sound of Benedict's voice brought the balm of relief.

'Victoria,' he sounded amiable, 'I'm sorry, I don't think I'm going to get back to the office. Are there any queries about the notes you're typing out?'

'No, I think we dealt with all that yesterday. You won't be back?' she prompted.

'No. After you left I had a call from Daniel Waldbeck asking me to meet him this afternoon to talk over one or two points.'

'Oh?' It was a breath of relief rather than a comment.

'Are you there, Victoria?'

'Of course.' There was a note of elation in her voice which she didn't mind him hearing.

'Then will you just go home at the usual time? I'll get back as soon as I can. Oh, and take that file back home, will you? Sorry to have given you a trip for nothing.' For Benedict he was unusually thoughtful and considerate.

'It was nothing.'

'Then I'll see you tonight. Goodbye, love.'

Victoria's sense of relief and euphoria lasted all of ten minutes before her normal instincts began to reassert themselves. Of course he had to give some explanation for his unexpected absence from the office. And if she hadn't known he had lunched with Camilla she could have accepted his story without any question. But suppose if after lunch they had gone back to the Baroness's flat in Eaton Gate. Victoria knew the address well enough as she had been called upon to have flowers sent there on several occasions in the last few months. Back to that luxurious, sybaritic flat. In her mind's eye she saw the draperies of hot pink silk on the walls, the tiger-skin rugs on the floors. She shuddered and put a hand to her forehead, and before she knew what she was doing she had lifted up the phone and was dialling a number.

'Hello. Daniel Waldbeck's office.' The familiar nasal voice came over the line.

'Oh, hello, Miriam.' Victoria's heart was beating uncomfortably fast and she tried to ignore the wretched feeling of guilt that had come sweeping over her. 'It's me, Victoria. I'm trying to contact Benedict and think he might be with Daniel.'

'Victoria? Well,' Miriam ignored the reason for the call, 'if you aren't the dark horse! I just got back to the office this morning and you could have knocked me down with a feather when Janey told me about you and Benedict. What does it feel like to be married to your boss?'

'I suppose it depends on your boss.' Victoria had been asked the question often enough to have developed an answer which seemed to satisfy.

'I bet,' Miriam said admiringly. 'Well, clearly I have the wrong kind of boss. Married with three kids and . . .'

'Did you have a good holiday?' Victoria interrupted. 'How was Mombasa?'

'It was great, just great. All right for a honeymoon, if that's why you're asking. Janey told me that you and Ben aren't going away till later and . . .'

'That's right.' Victoria interrupted Miriam's flow with the ease born of long practice but wondering for the umpteenth time just how a taciturn man like Daniel put up with such a garrulous secretary. 'You must tell me all about it some time. But if I could just have a word with Benedict. Unless they're in conference, of course.'

'But they're not here. That's what I'm trying to tell you, love. Daniel's in Edinburgh working on something with Scottish television. So wherever Ben is, it's not with Daniel. Now I wonder,' she sounded amiably reflective, 'did you say he told you he'd be with Daniel?'

'No, I didn't.' Victoria interrupted smoothly. 'I'll just have to phone around a bit. Sorry to have troubled you, Miriam.'

'No trouble. And what about having lunch one day? I was speaking to Barbara just about an hour ago and she was saying it was time we started our regular get-togethers again.'

'Lovely, Miriam,' Victoria replied insincerely. 'I'll give you a ring some time soon. Goodbye.' But when she replaced the receiver she sat for a long time gazing into space, the ache in her chest returned with such ferocity that she knew she was going to find it impossible to type any more that afternoon. In fact she didn't even know how she was going to cope with driving the car back to Peverell Square.

And of course when she arrived there it was a mistake to get involved in a row with Lumsden. It was always a mistake to have rows when you were overwrought and nervy, especially with a man like that. It had started with the usual silly trivial exchange of words when he found her in the kitchen making herself some tea.

'Good afternoon, Lumsden.' She spoke to him without turning when she heard the door leading to the garden open behind her.

'Good afternoon, madam.' His voice was cold with disapproval. 'You should have called me, madam, if you wanted your tea a little early.'

'Nonsense!' Her tone was less deferential than he was used to hearing. 'I'm quite capable of making some tea, Lumsden. Oh, and,' she watched him fetch a tray and begin to put china on it, 'don't trouble with that, Mr Gabriell isn't here.' She raised her cup to her lips and sipped. 'I don't suppose there's been a message from him?'

Deliberately it seemed he took his time in answering and bent to replace the tray in its slot by the side of the refrigerator. 'No, madam. But am I right,' his cold blue eyes taunted her, 'in thinking that he was lunching with the Baroness?'

'Yes.' Although she was seething with a mass of emotions Victoria thought she managed to conceal her feelings, only the very slight rattle of her cup as she put it down betraying her. 'Yes. Only lunch doesn't usually last till five o'clock, Lumsden. But,' she paused, determined to be as controlled as he invariably was, 'I'm glad you brought up the subject of the Baroness, Lumsden, because I want you to understand my feelings on the situation I found here this morning to be perfectly clear to you.'

'Your feelings, madam?' He made no attempt to hide the insolence in his tone, and this stiffened Victoria's resolve.

'In future, before you allow casual visitors the run of the house you will first obtain permission from Mr Gabriell or myself.'

'Indeed, madam?' Two red spots high on his cheeks indicated that perhaps he was less calm than he looked. 'Then you intend that I should turn away one of Mr Gabriell's oldest friends when she . . .'

'No, I'm not suggesting that. Although as you've been with Mr Gabriell less than a year I don't think you're in any position to make judgments about who are best friends and who are casual acquaintances. What I'm saying is no one is to have the freedom you allowed the Baroness without permission.'

'Really?' He was openly sneering now. 'And what makes you think I shall take any notice of what you say?'

Victoria realised there was nothing to be gained by getting into a vulgar slanging match with the man and turned to the door, but as she put her hand on the knob he got in his last vicious words, now spoken with a note of triumph. 'And what makes you think that I didn't have Mr Gabriell's permission?'

Only when she got back to the sitting-room did Victoria allow her feelings of despair to engulf her. She sank on to the soft velvet of the sofa, burying her face in her hands, and even when she heard the door open and sensed Lumsden's malicious eminence hovering over her, she made no attempt to look up.

'If I may give you a word of advice, madam,' now his voice was oily with synthetic concern, 'I shouldn't force Mr Gabriell to choose between us. I think, considering the relationship you have with him, that would be a very great risk.' Then he went out, closing the door behind him with professional quietness.

Emotional exhaustion must have made her fall asleep on the sofa and when she woke she found that she had been covered by the light folds of a mohair rug that was normally kept in the cloak-room. She stretched, for the moment unable to identify the sense of doom and despair that was weighing heavily, and even as she remembered a shadow fell across her face and, startled, she looked up into Benedict's face, unusually relaxed and friendly.

'You've had a good rest.' He held up a glass chinking with ice. 'I've had a tiring afternoon too and needed a pick-me-up. Join me?' He smiled and turned away, taking her reply for granted. 'Cinzano?'

'No, thank you.' Her mouth still felt dry and unpleasant after the wine she had taken at lunch. 'I'll have a tonic if you like.'

Apparently struck by something in her tone, he swung round to look enquiringly at her. 'All right.' A moment later he held out a tall crystal glass to her, watched while she put the rug aside and swung her legs on to the floor before putting out her hand to take the drink. Their fingers touched round the chilly surface and Victoria felt the stab of fire run through her body. She sensed his curious slightly narrowed gaze but refused to respond to it.

'I've given Lumsden the night off.' He sipped his drink, then with a faint sigh moved over to look out on to the garden.

'Oh?' The monosyllable was sharply questioning.

'Yes. I thought we might go out for a meal. There's a new place along the river and . . .'

'No.' Instinctively she knew that she wasn't going to make it easy for him to salve his guilt. 'I don't feel like going out tonight.'

'Don't you?' He watched her rise and stand in front of the empty fireplace where she felt less at a disadvantage. 'Don't you, Victoria?' Then he appeared to make an obvious effort. 'I just thought it might be pleasant to drive along the river . . . It's such a lovely warm evening. And,' he walked towards her, came close enough to be able to touch her, 'you look so pretty in that suit. It's new, isn't it?' Then when she didn't answer, 'I was afraid it would be crushed when I saw you lying there so peacefully, but it hasn't. Have you a headache or something?'

'No.' Deliberately she turned away from him. 'I just don't feel like going out. But I suppose as you've given Lumsden the evening off I'll be able to use the kitchen. If you're sure he won't object, that is.' She couldn't resist the gibe.

'What the hell does it matter whether he objects or not?' Although her eyes were on the toe of her green patent shoe tapping nervously on the high polished steel fender, she knew that his eyes had flashed dangerously. 'We don't have to ask him whether or not we can use the kitchen.'

'I wonder if *he* knows that.' Victoria felt her carefully controlled composure begin to slip. 'He seems to have the very firm impression that my wishes in the matter have very little to do with it.'

'So,' indulgent amusement was lurking below the surface of Benedict's reply, 'so that's what this moodiness is all about? You and Lumsden have had a row.' She heard him place his glass down beside hers on the mantelpiece, felt his hands on her shoulders pulling her back against him. 'Well, it doesn't matter. It will all blow over.' His face was against hers now, moving in what could have been an affectionate gesture, his voice was disarmingly, irritatingly gentle.

'I don't think so. Not this time.' A sob escaped her lips. 'He hates me.'

'Oh, Victoria!' Laughingly he turned her round

towards him. 'How can you imagine that? He
probably resents you a little. But why should he
hate you?' His hand came up to smooth her hair
back from her face, paused under her chin, turning
it firmly upwards. Gradually as they stared at each
other, his expression changed, the laughter faded,
the yellowish eyes seemed to darken, to reveal
depths of intensity that she had never seen before.
At the same time, one hand slipped down her back
moulding her trembling body against his.

'Victoria.' His husky voice spoke as the other
hand moved from her chin to the nape of her neck
where it stroked delicately, his mouth brushed
tenderly against hers.

For a moment all her instincts, all her longings
made her yearn to soften against the hard demanding strength of his body. Her lips parted
under his, the sudden sweetness of the joy she knew
was enough to wipe from her mind all the anguish
of the afternoon. Then unbidden into her mind
came a picture of a room she had never seen, all
soft pinkness and seductive tiger-skins. The ab-
surdity of it did not occur to her, but the anguish
struck her again. She knew Benedict too well to
allow him so easily to add her scalp to all the
others. The arms which had been on the point of
creeping round his neck stopped at his shoulders,
holding him politely, definitely away. Telling him
to go no farther.

'Victoria?' The faintly puzzled, almost disappointed note in his voice brought a surge of satisfaction to her throbbing heart.

'Well, as you assure me that I have a permit to
use the kitchen,' the light tone she used seemed to

bring a darkness to his expression, 'I'd better go and make myself useful. Luckily,' she gave a laugh which sounded shallow and glib, 'that's one of the wifely duties I am prepared to perform.'

'As you like.' His voice was tense with anger and as she went from the room she saw that he had turned away with a frown of impatience which was only too characteristic.

But the meal appeared to mellow him, and Victoria rejoiced in the skill that enabled her to show that as well as being a reasonably competent secretary she was a good enough cook. Not, she admitted, determined to be fair, that a great deal of cooking had been involved. The melon had been in the refrigerator, cool and perfectly ripe, the veal escallopes had required little preparation and less cooking and the courgettes had been easy too. The meal ended with biscuits and a variety of cheeses which Lumsden always chose with such care, but as she cleared away Victoria was glad to think that the burst of successful and rewarding activity had done her good, had taken her out of her mood of depression and misery.

'Can I help?' Benedict followed her into the kitchen carrying some of the dirty crockery.

'No, I can manage.' She was enjoying showing him how efficient and capable she was. 'I did some of the washing up as we went along.'

'Hmm.' He leaned against the doorway looking at her. 'I can see that there's more to you than meets the eye. Lumsden will definitely have to watch his step!' He disappeared for a moment, then came back, a long thin cheroot smoking between his teeth.

'*He* wouldn't believe that.' The glass of wine she had drunk increased her slight sudden euphoria. 'He thinks that if it came to a decision you would choose him.' She smiled at him, turning to throw off the jacket of her suit, leaving her with the brief figure-hugging blouse underneath. She quivered when she saw his quick warm glance sweep over her and mistook its significance.

'Lumsden thinks ... what?' His voice was very low and lazy.

'He thinks that if it came to a choice, a wife like me or a man like him,' quickly she rinsed the plates and stacked them in the rack, 'there would be only one result.' She giggled faintly, then, struck by the heavy silence, she glanced up to see Benedict stubbing out his cigar in a violent gesture.

'What on earth were you thinking about, having such a conversation with Lumsden?' His voice was tight, his face pale with fury.

'I ... I ...' Victoria hesitated, nervous of this reaction to the comment so casually revealed. Then as she sensed that it was she and not Lumsden being accused, her chin rose challengingly. 'It was he who made the remark,' she said coldly.

'Well, I don't suppose he volunteered the opinion. Obviously something led up to it.'

'Yes, of course.' Carefully she wiped down the sink and turned to dry her hands before going over to the coffee machine which she seemed to find extremely absorbing. 'Would you like it black or ...'

'For God's sake, Victoria ...' Benedict strode over to where she was standing and swung her roughly round towards him. 'I'm not the least bit interested in the damned coffee! I want to know what happened today to cause Lumsden to make such an entirely out of character remark.'

'Of course,' she flared at him in an attempt to dispel the effect of his touch, 'of course! I can see that even before you've heard what happened you'll have made up your mind.' An indignant sob welled inexorably into her throat and the tears stung behind her eyes. 'Whatever happened, no matter how rude Lumsden was to me, somehow it will be my fault, I'll have provoked him in some way and . . .'

'Don't be so childish!' He shook her once, then his hands dropped to his side. 'You're my wife and of course I'll support you against him, no matter who's right or wrong.' He glared at her, then with what she thought was an effort he put out his hand and touched hers, briefly since she pulled herself away from him.

'Well,' turning away, Victoria hugged her arms about herself and walked over to the long window that overlooked the kitchen garden, 'if you must know . . .' She hesitated, longing to confront him with her knowledge of his association with Camilla but nervous of the explosion of anger that she knew would be bound to follow. Her mind was a confused jumble of all the day's happenings, all misplaced and out of order so that as she searched for the right thing to say, the words were strangely elusive.

'Come on, Victoria. I *would* like to know. Get it over, then we can forget it.'

Perhaps it was the gentleness with which he spoke that made the tears suddenly gush into her eyes, tears that she brushed away with an angry gesture from both her hands. 'It wouldn't have happened if,' she sobbed, 'if you'd been honest with me. I can stand anything but lies.' Miserably she looked round at him, shivering in the warm air.

'Lies?' Sweeping dark eyebrows came together in a frown of concentration. 'I don't usually tell lies, Victoria. As a rule it's too much trouble. I think you'd better explain further.'

'If you'd told me the truth about where you were this afternoon.' Unable to stand the searching scrutiny of his eyes, she looked away, wondering how they had reached this hopeless, humiliating conversation. 'Then I wouldn't have had to check up.' In her emotion she didn't see the change in his expression. 'And I wouldn't have been so upset when I came home.'

'Check up?' The calm in his voice deceived her. 'What do you mean you had to check up, Victoria?'

'Well, I thought that perhaps you weren't with Daniel after all. So I rang up Miriam and she told me.'

'Told you what?'

'That Daniel was in Edinburgh. So then I knew you must be with the Baroness.'

Benedict closed his eyes, pressed one hand against them and stayed in that position for a moment. Then, 'I'm afraid you've lost me, Victoria. Even if I wasn't with Daniel why should that automatically mean I was with Camilla?'

'Because she told me so.' Triumph rose within her as the enormity of his treachery returned to her mind. Victoria took a deep breath as she

prepared to expose to him the depth of her knowledge, although she tried to keep the sound of
satisfaction from her voice. 'When I came back to
the house this morning for the file you had left
here, I found the Baroness upstairs with
Lumsden.'

'What are you suggesting?' His voice was stiff
with disgust.

'Oh, not that.' She smiled wanly. 'I'm sure she
sets her sights a little higher than that. No, she was
there looking for something she'd left behind,' she
hesitated, 'on some previous occasion.' Despite her
close scrutiny of Benedict's face there was no sign
of guilt or embarrassment. 'And she went out of
her way to tell me that you and she were lunching
together today.' She stopped, her breast rising and
falling rapidly, her eyes shining with unshed tears,
her cheeks flushed with emotion.

'And so . . .?' Benedict's voice was cool and disapproving.

'And so . . .?' she stammered. 'What do you
mean?' It was a terrible anti-climax to think that
she had lost the initiative, that somehow she was
in danger of becoming the accused once again.

'And so,' his voice was hard now, all gentleness
obliterated as if for ever, 'why should you imagine
that because I had lunch with the Baroness, I didn't
keep my appointment with Daniel?' There was a
lengthy pause while his eyes seemed to sear her
with their contempt. 'You said something about
checking up, I believe, about ringing Miriam to
find out if I really was with him, then judging me
with your tawdry little mind, depending on what
her reply was.' With an expression of disgust he

whirled away from her. 'So I imagine his office will be agog with this juicy little piece of gossip. Everyone knows what kind of reputation she has!'

'You must think me an absolute fool.' Somehow Victoria clung on to her shreds of self-respect, pulling them around her like a cloak.

'No, I've never thought you that,' he hissed at her between clenched teeth. 'But I did expect trust from you. That, it seems, is something I must do without in my wife.'

Victoria thought it best to ignore that. 'Of course I didn't tell Miriam why I was ringing. I know her as well as you do and my feelings are as much at risk as your own. Now,' firmly she walked to the door, 'I'm going to bed. If you want coffee you'll just have to get it for yourself. Oh, and don't forget to clean up the kitchen or you might find that Lumsden has put it out of bounds for you as well!' She pulled the door closed behind her with an angry little click that must leave him in no doubt about her feelings, then quickly ran upstairs to her bedroom.

She lay awake in the large bed watching the minutes on the clock beside her tick tediously round—eleven o'clock, twelve, one, two. Three she missed, but she was awake again at four and when she went downstairs in the morning she knew that her face showed the evidence of her disturbed night. Benedict raised his eyes from his newspaper as she went into the dining-room, said a brief good morning, then returned his attention to what he was reading as Lumsden came in with some fresh toast and coffee, greeting Victoria with the quiet deference he used in Benedict's presence. When he had closed the door softly behind him, Victoria cleared her throat and tried to speak.

'About last night, Benedict.' Her voice was thick with misery, but whatever she was about to say was lost when he pushed back his chair with a furious gesture and came across to her, throwing down the paper on to the table beside her.

'And you,' the words were hissed at her, 'have the impudence to follow me around, to spy on me! How dare you?'

'Benedict?' Bewildered, she gazed up into a face grown pale with a controlled anger. She followed the line of his eyes to where a long dark finger stabbed at the printed words of what was one of the most popular gossip columns in the country. *Lady Lavinia's Notebook*, it called itself, but everyone knew that Lady Lavinia was a group of so-called journalists who specialised in turning over stones in the hope of finding material to embarrass or titillate, preferably both. And if they were unlucky and found nothing they weren't above fabricating some piece of gossip which would be very interesting to their readers.

Victoria read swiftly, skimming through the first paragraph which alluded to a pop star who was doubtless glad enough of the publicity, although it was doubtful if the Bishop's wife referred to would be correspondingly grateful. If she existed.

Then Victoria felt her face grow hot, one hand went to her mouth and she bit nervously on her knuckles as she read.

So, the sexy Mr B ... G ... who was married so suddenly, so unexpectedly less than a month ago can't quite sever his connection with his former constant companion. He and the beautiful titled model had eyes only for each other when they lunched together yesterday at L ... But another pair of eyes found them an intriguing spectacle too, for in the opposite corner I was fascinated to see the bride, doing her best to be invisible. And her lunch date, so very anxious to be tête-à-tête with her, had to struggle to retain her attention. A truly astounding situation which I shall be studying closely in the days to come and about which I shall keep you informed.

When at last Victoria raised her eyes to look at Benedict, she revealed an expression in which guilt was mingling with dismay, but both were finally overcome by apprehension.

CHAPTER SEVEN

'I THINK, Victoria, that after our trip to Harrogate next weekend we'd better try to make up our minds about a holiday.' Benedict tossed aside the sheaf of papers he had been studying since they had finished dinner and lay back in his chair looking at her.

'Holiday?' Pushing the swathe of heavy hair back from her forehead, Victoria raised her head from the piece of embroidery she had been working on. In spite of herself the colour flowed into her cheeks, colour caused by the feelings of guilt and misery which had assailed her since that awful row they had had last week.

'Yes.' There was no relaxation in the grimness of his manner so that she knew that his suggestion in no way signified that he had forgiven or forgotten. 'We did say, when we married, that we would go away later. Now that I've got the TV programmes out of the way for the time being we ought to try to fit something in.'

The programme which had taken up so much of their time had been recorded at the end of last week and went out over the networks on Saturday night. They had sat together watching it, Victoria gazing hypnotised in the half-dark at the elegant charming man on the square screen who was cleverly, intelligently questioning one of the wiliest and most skilful Ministers in the Government. The fact that the politican was also a woman appeared to make her more responsive to his probing, so that at the end of the half hour the public had a much better idea of the gap between her party's aims and their achievements. But it was hard to equate the persuasive, relaxed chairman of the programme with the grim silent man who sat looking at his own performance. Even Victoria's warm congratulations were brushed aside as if they didn't matter.

'Is there anywhere you'd particularly like to visit?' The coldness of his voice interrupted her recollection and brought a pang of self-pity which was swiftly followed by a flash of anger.

'Not really. In fact with this present atmosphere existing between us I doubt the wisdom of going away at all.' Her voice quavered so that she caught her lower lips fiercely between her teeth. 'I'm dreading the weekend at Harrogate as it is. I'm wondering if it might be wiser to ring and tell Mother that I'm ill, that for some reason we can't come.' Her voice rose on a note of hysteria.

'Of course we can't do that.' Although his voice was calm she sensed somewhere inside him a tension that equalled her own. 'From what you say they've been making quite a lot of preparations, and we can't let them down now.' He reached across to the table and pulled a cigar from the box, flicking his lighter as he put it to his lips. 'I,' he pulled the smoke into his lungs, then exhaled slowly, 'I shall do my bit. Just as you did when we were down in Cornwall. You captivated my mother and Janet. We,' the tawny eyes surveyed her speculatively, 'shall ensure that your parents are equally convinced that their only daughter has made a sensible marriage.'

'Sensible!' With an explosion of rage Victoria screwed her work into a ball and threw it across the room where it fell down behind a large table lamp, jamming between the wall and the round dark green shade. *'Sensible!'* The word was thrown at him accusingly. 'If only it were as easy to persuade ourselves of that!' She found relief in her anger, consolation in the superiority she felt looking down at the half-reclining figure as it relaxed in the large soft chair.

'Do you still need persuading?' The words were lazily spoken, as if Benedict were really curious about her reaction.

She glared for a moment, then laughed, a bitter unamused little sound. 'You must be joking,' she answered crudely. 'And don't,' she mocked, misled by his mild look as he clenched the cheroot between his teeth, grinning slightly, 'please don't tell me that you don't need convincing.'

'Don't talk like that!' Suddenly a hand shot out gripping her tightly about the wrist.

'Why not?' she jeered. 'Don't you care for the truth?'

'I've told you before,' the powerful fingers about her wrist tightened, 'I don't mind it.'

'You're hurting me!' The words were hissed through clenched teeth.

'Ah yes, the typical female reaction when things begin to get out of hand. You're hurting me!' He mimicked her words, cruelly catching the intonation. 'But you and your sex are so much more subtle in your cruelties.'

'You know so much about us, don't you?'

'Yes.' Abruptly Benedict relaxed his grip so that

she was able to snatch her hand away, then as she stood rubbing her wrist she saw him stub out his cigar and get lazily to his feet. 'Yes, I suppose I do.' He smiled, his teeth white in the shadowy room taking her attention from his eyes to his mouth. 'But strangely,' he reached out linking his hands gently about her waist, 'since I knew you, Miss Kendall, I find there's more and more about your sex which I don't understand.'

'You surprise me.' Feeling his arms begin to pull her closer, Victoria resisted, leaning back from him, an expression of distaste on her face.

'But don't let us be diverted along any side alleys. You were asking me to persuade you that we had a sensible marriage.'

'I was asking for nothing of the kind!'

'Oh?' A raised eyebrow mocked her. 'I thought that was what it was all about. Could it be that I made a fundamental error in my assessment of you, Miss Kendall? That you're like so many other females at heart, despite your cool self-assured exterior?' Smiling impudently down at her, he slid one arm more tightly about her waist while pressing his free hand to the soft full curve of her breast.

Victoria drew in a sharp breath of sheer panic, all her bravado undermined by the trembling ecstasy that his touch brought.

'Your heart is beating wildly, Victoria.' His voice was low, his mouth against her cheek as he spoke. 'Almost as wildly as my own.' He took one unresisting hand and held it against the smooth cotton of his shirt where her fingers could feel the throb of his pulses. Trying to escape, they spread so that she felt his warm skin beneath her hand, the crisp curling hair where the shirt was open to the waist.

'Oh?' She trembled against him, raising her mouth to his searching lips, rejoicing in the liquid fire that reached deep into her very bones.

'Victoria.' Gently he moved his face against hers, the faint sting of his beard causing the most un-expected sensations to ripple through her body. 'Victoria.' He leaned back, looking down into her face. 'Has anyone ever told you how beautiful you look when you're angry?' For once he sounded unsure of himself.

She looked back at him, searching his expression for some indication of his mood, seeing what she took for mockery in the lift of the eyebrow, the faintly cynical twist of his mouth.

'Don't be corny!' The unpleasant retort brought a darkening of his expression which at once made her wish she had said something more sophisticated and to regret the slackening of his arms so that she was obliged to step away from him. 'And soft words are no answer.'

'No, perhaps you're right. It's a habit you have. But I was hoping that possibly they might break through the shell you use to protect you.'

'I do no such thing!' She laughed condescend-ingly. 'Why do men expect women to fall into their arms whenever they say a few flattering words?'

'They don't.' Benedict spoke matter-of-factly. 'And it's quite true, it was a corny remark. I can't think what came over me. You deserve better.'

Suspiciously she looked at him expecting to dis-cern the usual faintly derisive raised eyebrow but this time he was looking at her seriously, with an expression she couldn't fathom. An expression which threatened the fragile self-possession she had forced upon herself.

'We were talking about our marriage . . .'

'Which disappoints you.' It was a statement rather than a question.

'Can you say that it has lived up to your expectations?'

'Yes, I can.'

'What you mean is,' her voice shook slightly, 'you expected little.'

'No, I expect a great deal. The only thing is, Victoria, I didn't expect everything at once. I'm patient. I can wait for things to come right.'

'And you think they will?' she asked in a voice of passionate despair.

He didn't answer for a moment, then put out a hand to touch her cheek, this time with a gentleness wholly platonic. 'How many marriages do you imagine are perfect from the start? Do you think that the most conventional love match doesn't encounter tremendous stresses in the first weeks and months? Do you seriously imagine that there isn't a long period of adjustment in every marriage?'

'But they . . .' She broke off before she could say any more and stood biting her lip, absurdly conscious of his hand resting so casually against her skin.

'Ah yes, but they . . .' His hand dropped to his side, the note of mockery was back in his voice and his eyes when she looked at him. 'But they . . .' he repeated, telling her that he knew exactly what she had been about to say. 'I've been thinking, Victoria,' he turned away, picked up the cigar and she waited while he applied a light to the end, 'of what you said that day in Cornwall.' Slowly he blew out a column of blue smoke. 'And quite frankly,' he studied the glowing end with satisfaction, 'I've come to the conclusion that I don't accept your story.'

'My story?' she procrastinated, knowing exactly what he meant.

'Yes, your reason for marrying me.' Swiftly he raised his eyes, searching her face intently. 'I don't believe it was some half-formulated idea to pay me back, presumably for years of slavery as my secretary. No, Victoria,' his keen narrowed eyes were studying her discomforture, 'if life with me had been so bad you could have escaped years ago. There are plenty of vacancies for competent secretaries in London and I happen to know that John Hills held out a tempting offer to you a couple of years ago. So why didn't you take it?'

Victoria coloured. She had no idea that Benedict had known of John Hills' attempts to get her to go over to his publishing organisation, but she chose to ignore what she considered to be the red herring.

'Of course you don't believe me. I didn't expect you to.' She smiled condescendingly. 'It goes back to what I just said. Men never believe what offends their pride.'

'Nevertheless, my sweet, I think there was some other reason. Quite apart from the fact that I believe that I'm irresistible to women.' The words were spoken in a tone of self-mockery that relieved her of the need to be suspicious, but his next words caused her to search his face for some clue as to his meaning. 'But perhaps you had some other score to pay off.'

'That's nonsense. What other reason could there be apart from the one I told you about?'

'Another man, perhaps? Although you told me there was no one.'

'There was no one. Why should I . . .'

'Not even Iain?' he interrupted smoothly.

'So,' her eyes narrowed stormily, 'so you did listen in on the phone that day!'

'Mmm. Quite by chance, of course. I merely lifted the receiver because you appeared to be taking rather longer than usual to answer. I found it . . . interesting.'

'I despise people who eavesdrop on conversations!' Victoria snapped.

'Of course you do. But I was in rather an awkward position. I didn't want to come the heavy husband—get off the line and don't dare contact my wife again. Besides, the conversation seemed rather a personal one. I thought it a pity to interrupt.'

'It was personal,' she said coldly. 'All the more reason for letting me know that you were listening in. I certainly shouldn't have minded if I had known. There was nothing particularly private about it.'

'No?' He sounded sceptical. Then with an abrupt change of direction, 'I suppose it was Iain whom you took with you to spy at Lalo's?'

'I didn't spy on you—don't be so ridiculous! I wouldn't have known you were going out with the

Baroness if she hadn't thrown the fact in my face.'

'So you decided to get even with me by going out with Iain?'

'Of course not. You're free to meet the Baroness every day of the week. And she didn't tell me where you intended to eat. Quite simply it was a coincidence that we happened to go to the same place.'

'And a coincidence that "Lavinia" happened to be there with her notebook at the ready.' His voice was cold with disapproval now.

'You know these places so much better than I do. If you want your . . . your meetings kept quiet perhaps you should choose a less obtrusive rendezvous.'

'Then perhaps the very fact that I went there with Camilla meant that there it was was less important than you appear determined to imagine. No, it's your meeting with Iain I'm more concerned about.'

'Of course it is.' Victoria was quickly on the defensive. 'As always, there's a different law for men than for women. I mustn't do as you do, but do as you say.'

'Naturally.' There was a grimness about his mouth now. 'If there's one thing I will not tolerate, Victoria, that is gossip about my wife.'

She was so surprised that she almost laughed in his face. 'You won't tolerate that! But you expect me to put up with it.'

'You know what I think of gossip columns. They're a comfortable refuge for hacks who couldn't find a living any other way, and I suppose we're stuck with them until the British public develop a less prurient taste. All I'm saying is,'

Benedict spoke very quietly, 'I don't expect my wife to feature in them. I'll make allowance for this recent episode, put it down to your inexperience, but that's all.'

'Oh, all right.' Quite suddenly Victoria was wearied of the whole business, and it was hard to pretend that she disagreed with Benedict. People like him would always be at the mercy of gossip columnists, but it was wise to be as discreet as possible to avoid their attentions. Only she couldn't allow him completely to have the last word. 'Of course, it all began because of my finding the Baroness here that day. Knowing everything, being on such friendly terms with Lumsden. There's a limit to my tolerance as well as yours.'

'That won't happen again, Victoria—I'll see to it. And,' he got up suddenly and walked over to the sideboard from which direction came the comforting sound of ice clinking against glass, 'about Lumsden—I've been thinking.' He handed her a glass of Cinzano without having asked if she wanted it. 'Perhaps some time in the near future you might prefer to give up work, stay at home and be a housewife.' The yellow eyes raked her face.

'You mean,' carefully controlling the tremor that threatened to spill the liquid down her dress, Victoria placed the glass on the table at her elbow. 'You mean, you'd like to find another secretary.'

'Of course I didn't mean that. I'm simply suggesting that maybe,' he emphasised the words, 'some time in the future you might be happy to escape from the rat-race. Stay at home and do the cooking—I know you can, because you told me as much yourself.'

'And Lumsden?' She raised the glass to her lips, looking at him intently over the rim. 'I couldn't bear to be in the house all day with him.'

'Oh, Lumsden. Well, I've never been entirely happy about him from the beginning. And I've had a word with him about his attitude to you and . . .'

'You've . . . you've what?' Victoria was suffused by a feeling of overwhelming warmth and comfort. 'You mean you believed me?'

'Of course I believed you. Why shouldn't I?' He laughed shortly. 'And I think Lumsden got the message and soon he'll be thinking of moving on.'

'Oh, Benedict, thank you! I really would be much happier if he weren't here. I feel,' she put her arms round herself, 'I feel he's disliked me from the first.'

'Well, you do what you like. Perhaps it would be better if you were at home. And to tell the truth,' he grinned boyishly at her, 'I'm one of those old-fashioned guys who prefer his women in the house. Now,' he reached out a hand for the batch of papers he had tossed down earlier, 'we'd better return to the subject of that holiday. There seem to be two choices—a busy holiday with everything organised, or a lazy one lying on a beach in the sunshine.'

'Oh, an organised one.' Victoria spoke quickly without really thinking further than the in-advisability of spending too many long empty hours together, then at once regretted it when she saw his knowing cynical look switch from her face to the papers.

'Ye—es.' It was a long speculative word. 'You're right of course Victoria.' His smile was faint. 'I seem to have spent the evening saying that. My secretary would say such submissiveness is quite outside my character. Then,' he frowned, 'it looks like three weeks studying the Hindu temples of India. Or perhaps you would prefer looking at the bird life in the High Andes? How does that strike you, my sweet? Or,' without waiting for an answer he went on, 'Israel perhaps—two thousand years of Christian history, all in eighteen days. Mmm, sounds interesting.' He raised his eyes unexpectedly but seemed to notice nothing of the dismay written so clearly on her face. 'They all sound fascinating, don't they?' Idly he turned over the pages. 'Of course, they aren't on the usual package tour itineraries.'

'Fascinating,' she echoed in a flat tone.

'Well, will you leave it to me, Victoria? I'll sort something out.'

'Of course.'

'Hm, I've just noticed this one. The churches and museums of Moscow and Leningrad. Now there they really do keep you on the go all the time.' The face he raised to hers was filled with enthusiasm. 'That might just be the answer, Victoria. Yes,' he pulled a little pad towards him and began to scribble, 'I'll make some more enquiries about this tomorrow.'

'Well, I'm feeling rather tired.' Victoria got up from her chair and walked over to retrieve her sewing from behind the lamp. 'I think I'll go to bed.'

'Yes. Goodnight, love.' Benedict spoke abstractedly without raising his eyes from the papers.

But as she closed the door behind her she imagined that she heard the sound of stifled laughter. And then his voice called her name, a note of excitement in it.

'Yes?' The movement of the door was arrested as she waited for him to go on.

'I've just noticed—fifteen days in Berber tents following the ancient slave routes of Morocco. A holiday that you will remember for the rest of your lives, it says here.'

'Definitely not! I haven't been in a tent since I was in the Guides. I hated it then and I'm sure I'll hate it now. Especially Berber tents!' And this time Victoria banged the door and stalked upstairs without waiting for an answer.

But later, as she lay in the softness of the double bed, her lips curved into a smile as she realised that she had been having her leg pulled. Berber tents indeed! She sighed. She could just about put up with the Hindu temples. Or even the birds of the Andes. But why had she been such a fool as to say she would like a busy holiday? When her idea of heaven was lying for a fortnight on the beach at Benidorm. With Benedict. She groaned and turned round to press her face into the pillow.

It was a perfect day as they sped north on the M1. When they left the congestion of the city behind them they settled down to a steady cruising speed Benedict relaxed with his arm along the seat behind her. In the last day or two he had been so kind, so charming that she was trembling with the emotion she felt for him. If she had ever had any idea that propinquity would cure her of the wild feelings she had harboured for him over the years, then she had been wrong. Terribly, gloriously wrong.

But as they drew closer to Yorkshire Victoria felt another tension and excitement begin to gnaw at her stomach. She knew that Benedict had been working himself, and her, into the proper mood for their visit, into some kind of convincingly amiable frame of mind which would reassure her mother and father. But what if they should see through the façade, sense that there was something not quite normal about their marriage.

After all, they must have had their suspicions about that already. Many times since the event she had shuddered at the shock she had inflicted on her poor mother. The words she had spoken to Benedict on the day of their wedding had returned to her mind time and time again since then. She would hate it if her daughter did the same thing.

Her daughter—how unlikely it seemed! And yet she supposed at some time in the future she and Benedict would have children. He would make the decision that the time had come and that would be that. It would be nice to imagine that when the moment arrived she would be able to resist him, politely, insisting that he should wait until she made up her mind about the matter. But she very much doubted that the time would ever come when she could reject him. He would have only to crook his little finger and she would be running into his arms. Throwing herself at her own husband! Her face burned with the torment of her feelings and she looked round in bewilderment when she realised that the car was coming to a halt.

Benedict's face was looking down at hers with

understanding. 'Feeling uptight, love?' He reached across to release her seat-belt, then kept his hand on her waist.

She nodded, wishing that her thoughts hadn't been so instantly confirmed by his lightest touch.

'Don't be. It'll be all right. I'll be very good, you'll hardly recognise me. And they definitely won't. They certainly won't be able to understand all those letters you wrote about the slavedriver you had to work for.'

'Oh, Benedict!' She coloured, although her lips curved into a faint smile. 'I just feel so awful. When I think what a shock it must have been to them. How could I?' She cried the words despairingly.

'Well, you can blame me for that. And anyway, from what you say the party they've arranged for tomorrow night is to be almost like a wedding reception. And you've bought a glamorous new dress, haven't you?'

'Yes. As Mum seemed so determined I thought I'd better. I'm trying so desperately to make up for everything, and . . .'

'And I'm going to help you.' Unexpectedly he pulled her close to him so that she felt the breath was being squeezed out of her body. His mouth crushed against hers, fierce and demanding for a moment before suddenly he held her at arm's length, giving her a little shake as if he were amused at himself. 'And I promise that if I don't have your mother eating out of my hand at the end of the weekend, then I'll begin to think I'm losing my touch!'

But it wasn't just her mother whose reservations were instantly swept away, for Mr Kendall seemed equally and immediately at ease with his son-in-law. Victoria, hearing them discuss golf over pre-lunch glasses of sherry, looked at Benedict in surprise.

'I didn't know you played.'

Rather than answer her, Benedict turned to Mrs Kendall. 'All these years and still she doesn't know! It isn't very encouraging.'

'But you've never mentioned golf to me!' Victoria spluttered, halfway between amusement and indignation.

'She's never asked me. Not once,' Benedict explained to his mother-in-law.

'Tut, tut, Victoria!' The girl watched in dismay as her mother fluttered her eyelashes. 'You really ought to do better than that. After all, a man has to be pampered. Look at the way I've taken care of your father all these years.'

Solemnly Mr Kendall looked across at his daughter and closed one eye. Each of them knew that Victoria's mother was much more interested in work on charity committees than anything as mundane as caring for a house and was perfectly happy to leave that side of things to a series of capable daily women.

'Anyway,' now she was looking like a cat who had swallowed the cream, 'just take Benedict for a walk round the garden, dear. There's just time before lunch and I must just go and see that things are all right in the kitchen.'

'Off you go, then.' Mr Kendall went over to the sideboard and began to refill his glass. 'Sure you won't have another, Benedict?'

'Positive.' Benedict slipped his arm about his

wife's waist quite as if he enjoyed having it there. 'I find the idea of a walk round the garden very attractive.'

'Oh, and——' Mr Kendall seemed to hesitate, 'have a look at the old tennis court, Victoria.'

'The old tennis court,' she mused aloud as they walked down the flight of shallow steps leading from the french doors. 'What on earth can he mean by that?'

'I very much suspect, my sweet.' Benedict's voice was dry and he seemed to have forgotten any ideas of charm, 'I very much suspect that your mother had no intention of being done out of a proper wedding reception for her only child.' And there, in front of Victoria's incredulous gaze, the doors tied back so that the pink and white hangings were clearly visible, was a white marquee, gleaming in the bright sunshine, its sides billowing in the faint breeze.

The protests which Victoria made during lunch were surprisingly mild and easily brushed aside by her mother.

'Nonsense, darling.' She watched her husband carve the joint of beef and held out a hand for the plate. 'In any case, I don't mean to argue about it. You had your own way about your wedding, you must allow Daddy and me to have some fun now.' She spooned some new potatoes, carrots and peas on the plate and handed it across to Benedict.

'Now don't involve me in this, Joan.'

Mrs Kendall ignored her husband's interjection. 'And besides, I want to show you both off to all our friends. It's not everyone's daughter who marries a television personality.'

'He doesn't like being known as that, Mother.'

'Well,' Joan Kendall smiled approvingly at her new son-in-law, 'I know he won't mind this once and I'm sure he'll enjoy all the excitement as much as we shall.'

'Of course I shall, Mrs Kendall. I think it was a wonderful idea.'

'Well,' Victoria looked at her husband in astonished indignation, 'you really are the most contrary creature!' The words were spoken in the affectionate tone they had been maintaining since their arrival. 'All that nonsense about keeping the whole thing such a secret, and then letting the press know at the last minute! And now you're acting as if *you've* been deprived of a proper wedding!'

'You're right, of course, Victoria. And I admit I was wrong. I only wish you'd persuaded me to change my mind at the time.' Without seeming to notice his wife's look of vexation Benedict turned to his mother-in-law. 'It's a super meal, Mrs Kendall. I'm glad I had the sense to marry a girl whose mother is a good cook.' And he grinned across the table at Victoria, totally oblivious of the expression of withering scorn with which she responded.

It was early afternoon before they had to face the embarrassing moment which Victoria had been dreading since they had left their own home that morning. Mrs Kendall coming back from a consultation in the kitchen suggested casually that perhaps if Benedict cared to bring in their cases they would like to go upstairs to their bedroom.

'Yes, thanks, Mrs Kendall.' Obediently Benedict rose, reaching into the pocket of his jacket for his keys. 'I'll just get them.'

'Let me help you.' Victoria's father made a half-hearted attempt to lever himself out of his favourite chair beside the open window.

'No—really.' Benedict held up a hand firmly. 'Don't get up. There's only two cases and I can manage easily.'

'Oh well, if you insist.' He smiled at his daughter and yawned. 'I must say it's very pleasant to lie here and not to have to rush back to the office as usual. I'll just doze off for a moment, so when you all come back in don't bang any doors.'

Victoria followed her mother upstairs without waiting for Benedict to bring the cases, dismissing her mother's query with a casual shake of the head.

'Oh, I think he's quite capable of finding his way upstairs, Mother. Where are we, by the way?' They paused on the wide half-landing to look out of the large stained glass window overlooking the wide drive which swept up from the road towards the house.

'I've put you next door to us, darling. We just had the room done up in the spring—I think I told you at the time. And there are plenty of cupboards and space in that one.'

'Oh.' Victoria was feverishly thinking that the room was exactly next to the one occupied by her parents, and although in the old-fashioned house with thick walls the sound-proofing was good she knew that every time she spoke she would be conscious of their nearness. 'I like the wallpaper, Mother.' Her pleasure in the pink and mauve roses was genuine enough. 'And the new carpet.' She looked down at the deep pile, nudging it with her open-toed sandal. 'Thank you, Mother.' Impulsively she put her arms round the older woman, holding her close for a moment before the sound of Benedict pushing open the door parted them.' The room is lovely!'

'I'm glad you like it, darling.' Her mother's eyes were suspiciously bright as she looked from one to the other. 'It's wonderful to see you both so happy.' And she went out, closing the door softly behind her.

Victoria felt the colour rise in her cheeks as she bent over the large red case which Benedict had laid on the bench at the foot of the bed. She tried to pretend that his eyes weren't on her as she shook out the folds of the cream silk dress which she had bought for the following day's party, then felt relief as well as a curiously perverse disappointment when he turned away and stood looking out of the large bay window which overlooked one corner of the garden.

'I had no idea,' she spoke only when she felt that the continuing silence threatened to choke her, 'that they would go to these lengths.' Unwillingly she walked over to the window to stand beside him where together they could look down at the rose beds with at one side, the flat clipped grass of the old tennis court and the marquee. 'It seems slightly ridiculous.'

'So long, my sweet.' There was a faint touch of the familiar asperity in his manner now. 'So long as you don't expect me to slip down to the marquee tonight. What you said the other night about tents goes for me too.' His eyes went over to the large

double bed which had seemed to dominate the
room since their arrival. 'Tonight I mean to sleep
there. I suggest it's your turn to do the decent
thing.' To Victoria his smile seemed particularly
cruel, the expression in the tawny eyes so especially,
so blatantly speculative that nothing could have
prevented her answering as she did.

'As you said when we were in Cornwall,' she
drawled with a cutting edge to her voice, 'I shall
take great care not to disturb you. The only difference between us, Benedict, is that you obviously
couldn't trust yourself.' The words were an in-
spiration which had suddenly flown into her mind.
'I shan't have that problem, and you will be perfectly safe.' She walked over to the door, pausing
only when the heavy brass knob rested firmly in
her palm. 'Oh, and the bathroom is across the
landing—the next door to the small window.' The
triumph of having once again had the last word
lasted her all the way to the top of the stairs.

CHAPTER EIGHT

AND despite her bravado throughout the rest of the day Victoria could not divert her mind from the thoughts that were so disturbing to her. During the afternoon, when she spent some time in the kitchen with her mother and Mrs Paige completing some of the preparations for the party which was to take place the following evening, she was remembering Benedict's words and the smart-alecky way she had answered him. That made it all the more strange that she should jump so nervously when his voice sounded in her ear as she was stirring a small saucepan on the stove.

'What are you doing?' He leaned his face against her cheek, making her catch her breath. Then she remembered that Mrs Paige was standing at the large table in the centre of the room and she understood the display was for public consumption.

'I'm cooking the filling for some fruit tarts for tomorrow. You've met Mrs Paige,' she waved the saucy wooden spoon vaguely, then found her hand held still while Benedict scooped some of the cream in his forefinger and took it to his mouth.

'Mmm, super!' He smiled his charming smile at the woman who was rolling out pastry. 'Yes, Mrs Paige and I know each other. I've already told her how much I enjoyed the lunch.'

'Well, she's a wonderful cook.' Victoria wrinkled her nose at him as if they were the best of friends. 'And if you must know, she taught me, and Mummy too. But neither of us will ever be able to make pastry the way she does. It's a highly secret family recipe and she's making half a dozen cases for tomorrow and then we'll fill them with this and top with fruit.' She transferred her attention to the pot, studying the thickness of the mixture gravely. 'There, I think that's ready.' She removed the pot from the heat and continued to stir, watching Benedict with a sardonic expression. 'And now I must stir it till it cools.'

'You look quite the part.' A moment later he had transferred his attention to Mrs Paige as she gently eased the pastry into a flan ring. 'You know I'm trying to persuade Victoria to give up work in the office and to stay at home instead.'

'That's where she should be.' Mrs Paige, although often uncommunicative, had uncompromising opinions. 'Too many women going out to work these days, that's half the trouble.'

Victoria took advantage of Mrs Paige's absorption in her task to raise an eyebrow in Benedict's direction. From past experience she knew that all Mrs Paige's rules applied to other people only. It never occurred to her to imagine that somewhere lurked an unemployed man who might be capable of doing her job. 'There's men's work and there's women's work', was another of her sayings, and even as Victoria thought of it she heard it being stated with the usual authority.

'There's men's work and there's women's work.' Clearly she had heard from her employer about

Lumsden. 'And I don't think housework is what men should be doing.'

'I'm sure you're right,' Benedict agreed smoothly. 'And I would like to think of Victoria being at home, putting my slippers to warm beside the fire at nights.' He darted a mischievous glance in his wife's direction. 'It's not much fun when we both have to dash out in the mornings and don't get back till after six.'

'Fun!' Mrs Paige spoke in a tone of mild reproof. 'Who said life was meant to be fun?' Victoria had heard this before too and turned away to hide her smile as Mrs Paige came across the floor with three pies ready to go in the oven. 'But I will say,' as she straightened up she cast an appraising eye at Benedict's tall lounging figure, 'I think Victoria could have done worse. By a long chalk,' she added with a vague hint of regret. 'I wasn't prepared to be easily won over. It was such a shock for everyone and Mrs Kendall, poor soul, was in a real state. But then young ones are so wilful these days. In any case,' now it was Victoria who was the subject of her disapprobation, 'I was beginning to think that she was being too particular. You're not the first one that she's had here. Although,' she gave a faint smile at her own daring, 'although you're the first one she's been married to as far as I know.' The smile faded quickly. 'But now that I've met you, I'm glad.'

'Thank you, Mrs Paige. That means a lot to me.' There was no sign of mockery as he put his arm lightly round the elderly woman's shoulders. 'And next time I come up you'll have to tell me about all those other men Victoria's had here. That's not the impression that she gave me, you know.'

A few moments later they left Mrs Paige mixing another lot of pastry and strolled together across the wide hallway.

'Well,' his head turned towards her and she knew that she was being mildly taunted, 'I'm glad someone is pleased! Even if it is only the house-keeper.'

'Oh,' Victoria determined that for the rest of their visit she would not allow him to get under her skin, 'you needn't worry about that. They're *all* absolutely delighted. And you can rest assured that you haven't lost your touch. Not in the least.' As she spoke the last words she turned in the doorway to smile at him—and was surprised to recognise there a flash of something that looked very much like anger. Though why he should be angry with what she had said she quite simply had no idea.

In response to Mrs Kendall's assertion of total exhaustion they decided that evening to save cooking by going out to a pub for a meal.

'Although,' complained Benedict as he waited for his mother-in-law to settle down in the rear seat of the car, 'after that huge lunch I really don't need any more to eat.' He climbed into the front seat next to the driver. 'You know that Victoria and I aren't used to eating at midday. A pot of yoghurt and a cup of black coffee, that's what I'm allowed when I'm in the office.'

'That's to make up for the times when you eat out,' his wife reminded him sweetly. 'All those so-called business lunches!'

The tawny eyes narrowed in her direction before

switching to the older woman. 'I was telling Mrs Paige that I'd like to have Victoria stay at home. Will you help me persuade her?'

'Of course.' Mrs Kendall turned her attention to her daughter. 'If that's what you want, darling.'

'It's what Benedict wants.' Victoria shrugged almost imperceptibly. 'So long as he allows me to choose his new secretary.'

Mrs Kendall laughed. 'What's she to be, fat and forty?'

'Or even married. His last secretary was married. I . . .'

'Don't say any more, darling,' the interruption from the front seat was drawling, 'or I might begin to think you're jealous!'

'Of course she's jealous. And who has more right to be jealous?' Mrs Kendall teased. 'She knows only too well what can happen between the boss and secretary. I'm right, aren't I, Victoria?'

'You are, Mother.' The reply was laconic, then as if she were suddenly interested in the scenery Victoria sat forward, leaning over the seats between the two men. 'Oh, Daddy, it's years since I've been out this way. Remember how we used always to come here for picnics on Sundays?'

'Yes.' Mr Kendall gestured to the side of the road where the ground fell away towards a river which could be seen gleaming, then disappearing through clumps of trees at the foot of the valley. 'Down there, Benedict, we spent many an hour when Victoria was small. She was a real tomboy then, happiest when she had a fishing net in her hand or a cricket bat. I used always to say she ought to have been a boy.'

'I'm rather glad she's not.' Although Benedict didn't trouble to turn round with his mocking stare Victoria felt her cheeks growing warm, and her mother's complacent expression did nothing to ease the embarrassment she felt. She was annoyed with Benedict that he should go to so much trouble to assure her parents that their relationship was very much secure, and was about to lie back in her seat gazing sulkily out of the window when his hand came up to touch her bare arm where it leaned on the back of the seat. It was an intimate little gesture, the kind that happily married people indulged in without thinking. And that was exactly the impression Benedict was giving now—that he scarcely noticed what he was doing. And yet his touch brought an emotion flaring into her blood, her heart hammering into her throat so that if she had wanted to she could not have moved away from him. The feeling was too exciting, too compulsive for her ever to want to end it.

'Here we are.' It was her father's hearty voice that brought the trembling moments to an end as he drove into the car park of the small country pub. 'Do you recognise it, Vicky?' He looked round in expectation and at the same moment Benedict's hand moved away. 'I can see she doesn't.' Mr Kendall smiled triumphantly at his wife. 'I told you she wouldn't.'

'Of course you do.' Her mother swung her legs out of the door which Benedict was holding open for her. 'Don't you remember we came here once with the Westmacotts and . . .'

'Oh, of course.' As she felt the warmth in her face Victoria deliberately turned away from

Benedict's searching gaze, talking over her shoulder to the others as she stood looking at the long low stone building on the escarpment overlooking the River Wharfe. 'But it's been extended a lot, surely. It was just a tiny little pub then. Now it looks well into the country club style.'

'Yes.' Mrs Kendall came forward, slipping her hand into her daughter's arm as they walked ahead of the men towards the wide mahogany and glass door of the pub. 'Like all the old pubs round about. They become popular and then the owners are almost forced to expand. It's a pity really, because they seem all to have become the same in the last few years.' They stood and waited for the men to join them before going inside. 'Yes, it's changed a lot since we were here that day.' She waited until they were inside and comfortably settled at a round table by a wide window where they had a stunning view of the sun setting over the western side of the valley. Victoria pretended to be immersed in the menu, although really she had little appetite and was conscious only of the dark face opposite, making polite conversation with her father. And when they had chosen from the menu her mother returned to the subject that Victoria had hoped was comfortably behind them.

'Can you remember, Vicky,' she appealed to her daughter, 'that day we came with the West-macotts—was Iain with us? Daddy says no, but I think he was and . . .'

'No,' Victoria interrupted, her eyes firmly fixed on her mother's, ignoring the tawny ones watching, listening so assiduously. 'It was just the five of us.' She hoped that would be the end of the subject, but Benedict with deliberate provocation leaned back in his chair, one arm loosely dangling over the back, all his polite attention now directed towards his mother-in-law.

'The Westmacotts?' He frowned, trying to remember. 'Iain? I seem to remember the name.'

'Oh, you'll have heard Victoria talk about them. They're very good friends of ours and Iain is their nephew. Of course you'll be seeing them all tomorrow night. They're all dying to meet you. Iain is so sorry he missed you that day he met Victoria in London.' She darted a questioning, teasing glance at her daughter. 'Haven't you told Benedict about Iain, darling? You . . .'

'There's absolutely nothing to tell, Mother.' Victoria looked up in gratitude as the waitress came over and put a plate in front of her and waited until the others were served, but even this diversion was not going to deflect Benedict from a subject which interested him.

'No, she hasn't told me anything about Iain. And . . .'

'You know I saw him last week.' The eyes looking across the table were dark and stormy.

'Yes, I should hope she told you that.' Mrs Kendall spoke as if there was little doubt about it.

'. . . And,' Benedict continued as if he hadn't heard the interruptions, 'I would like to hear about all these other men in her life. The ones Mrs Paige told me about.'

This time it was Mr Kendall who took up the challenge. 'Oh, so Mrs Paige has been telling tales, has she, Victoria? Spilling all the beans about your lurid past?' The lightness of his manner brought a smile to Victoria's lips.

'Yes, wasn't it awful of her? And till then Benedict thought he was the only man in my life.' Deliberately she took up her spoon and began to eat the iced soup. 'I think it was too bad of her to disillusion someone as easily shocked as Benedict.' She flicked her long dark lashes up, intrigued to see that there was an answering gleam of amusement in his eyes. 'But now,' she shook back her hair so that she could look threateningly at each of them in turn, 'that's enough of my past or I'll begin to ask all of you questions about yours. And then the fat would really be in the fire!'

It was peaceful driving home along the quiet country lanes in the darkness of that evening in late summer—so peaceful, so contented that there seemed to be little need for conversation. Benedict and Victoria sat in the opposite corners of the rear seats, as Mrs Kendall had belatedly decided that perhaps they would prefer to sit together, each deep in the thoughts that were not for sharing.

But Victoria could not have said what jumble of reflections and emotions filled her mind on that drive home. To be so close to Benedict, to be able to see without moving her eyes from the tunnel of light towards which they were propelled in the darkness, the shadowy outline of his face, the light blur where his hand lay against the seat. So close that it would have been infinitely easy to move suddenly and make their fingers meet in an unexpected brief encounter. The thought brought her heart hammering again into her throat, the trickle of desire threaten to become a raging torrent. Then just as something outside her will impelled her hand to move towards his she saw that he had changed his position with a sad weary little sigh. And all at once it was too late for they were driving through the lighted streets of the town, circling the Stray and then stopping at the front door of the house.

'I'm going to make some more coffee, Victoria.' Her mother bustled towards the kitchen.

'Not for me, Mother, I'm tired.' She stood with her hand on the banister, one foot raised to the first step, refusing to look towards where Benedict waited by the front door, a sombre unfriendly figure until he turned with a smile for his father-in-law.

'Come on, Benedict.' His tone was for such a quiet man boisterous. 'Come on into my den and we'll have a last drink. I missed having one with my meal and . . .'

'Oh, aren't you having coffee?' Mrs Kendall reappeared in the kitchen doorway. 'I've just put on the kettle.' She looked from one of them to the other.

'No. Benedict and I are going to have a nightcap.' Firmly Mr Kendall turned towards the door of his study. 'After all, this really is like a stag night, and I think we've made concessions to the womenfolk already. What do you say?'

Benedict gave a slight shrug and a grin in his mother-in-law's direction, then went after his host. But just as he was about to follow him through the doorway he paused and turned to have a last word with his wife. 'I'll be up in half an hour, darling.' Their eyes met and Victoria could not escape the warning she read in the tawny gaze. She held her breath for a moment until the door closed with a decisive little click that seemed to underline his warning.

'You're sure you won't have a cup of coffee before you go upstairs, darling? Or maybe you'd like me to bring one up to you when you're in bed?'

'No, Mother, thank you.' Impulsively Victoria went over to the doorway where her mother still stood. 'And thank you for everything.' She put her arms round her, bending to press her cheek against the older woman's hair. 'For being so . . .' her voice quivered dangerously, '. . . so understanding about . . .' Close to tears that she dared not admit to, she bit her lip fiercely.

'Oh . . .' Mrs Kendall too appeared to be affected by the situation. 'Oh, it was hard at the time.' Releasing herself from her daughter's arms, she searched in her pocket for a handkerchief. 'But now that we've met Benedict we're beginning to understand. He's the kind of man we've always hoped you would marry. And tomorrow we're going to make up for the party we missed. As you said, it's definitely been a wedding with a difference, and there's no reason why we shouldn't celebrate belatedly. Oh dear,' she blew her nose fiercely, then laughed, 'there's the kettle boiling now.'

'It's switching itself off. Shall I make your coffee, Mummy?'

'No. I think I'll be just like you, darling.' With a quick glance round the kitchen Mrs Kendall switched off the light and walked with her daughter to the stairs. 'After all, tomorrow's going to be a hectic day and I suppose we'll need all the sleep we can get.'

They reached the top of the stairs and stood for a moment smiling at each other almost shyly before Mrs Kendall leaned forward to press a swift kiss on her daughter's cheek. 'Goodnight, then, darling. And you can say goodnight to Benedict for me.'

'Yes. Goodnight, Mother.' Victoria yawned ostentatiously. 'And to Daddy. If I'm not asleep by the time Benedict comes up I'll tell him.'

'I do hope they don't spend the whole night down there.' Mrs Kendall sounded faintly cross. 'You know what your father's like,' she said unfairly before she closed the door of her room.

Victoria sat looking at herself in the mirror of the dressing-table as she brushed her hair with long sweeping strokes. Once, when she thought she heard the sound of voices from downstairs her heart increased its already passionate tempo. Then there was silence once more and she rose, looking at herself in the thin cotton nightdress which left her shoulders bare and clung softly. Again she heard voices downstairs soon after the sound of a door opening, then footsteps coming steadily upstairs, another door opening and closing.

A sob burst from her throat and impulsively she crossed to the window, holding aside the heavy folds of the curtain, leaning her burning cheeks against the coolness of the wall. Her eyes saw nothing when they looked out into the darkness, then her attention was caught by the flare of a match. Briefly she saw her husband's face illuminated as he put the light to the tip of his cigar. Then slowly, the glow moving to and from his lips, he walked along the garden path.

All at once Victoria's excitement, her passionate expectation was subdued, was wiped out and replaced by a despair more devastating than any she had yet experienced. Obviously, he was determined to give her plenty of time so that she would be asleep before he came up to bed. He had no intention of allowing the intimacy of the double bed to undermine his plans.

Well, she decided in a sudden excess of fury, if that was what he wanted then that most certainly was what she wanted. She rushed across the room and threw herself into the bed, pulling the covers about her shoulders and switching off the light at her side of the bed. She lay for a moment staring into the room, still softly lighted from the shaded lamp at the other side of the bed, her heart still aching from all the changing emotions of the last few hours. Then with another impetuous decision she took one of the pillows from beneath her head and pulling back the covers arranged it down the middle of the bed.

The absurd action gave her a brief feeling of triumph and she lay back, satisfied that she had had the last word. But then the childishness of the action struck her like a blow so that she knew she could never bear him to know that she was capable of such behaviour.

And then, just as she was about to sit up and rearrange the bed as it had been before, she heard the sound of the bedroom door being pushed softly open. And with a pang she knew that she had left it too late. Now she had no choice but to pretend that she was sound asleep. She began to breathe deeply, evenly.

CHAPTER NINE

THE greatest surprise of the following day was the wholly unexpected arrival of Benedict's mother and Janet in the middle of the afternoon. Mr Kendall had gone off in the car with the excuse that he wanted to pick up some papers from the office, but when he returned shortly afterwards with the two women it became clear enough that his true destination had in fact been the railway station.

Victoria, who had been kneeling on the floor in the sitting-room struggling with a corner of the Chinese carpet which she had inadvertently kicked as she came into the room, dislodging the edge from under the leg of a heavy bookcase, looked up as she heard the sound of their arrival in the hall. It was only when she heard Benedict's voice, deep and warm and slightly amused, greeting his mother, that she had any indication of the identity of the arrivals.

But before she had time even to scramble to her feet the door was pushed open and her mother led Helen and Janet into the room, while behind them, his face sombre and dark as he looked down at her, was her husband. Victoria had to concentrate hard to be able to drag her eyes from his and to smile warmly at the two new arrivals.

'What a wonderful surprise!' As she got to her feet she made an attempt to push down the hem of the blouse which had escaped from the waist of her jeans. 'I had no idea . . .' She put her cheek against Helen's, then turned to Janet.

'It was planned only a few days ago.' Mrs Kendall, obviously pleased with the success of her plan, led her visitors into the room and waved them to seats. 'We decided . . . Daddy and I,' she explained to her daughter, 'that as this was to be your wedding, your real wedding,' she babbled happily, 'that other one in London didn't count, and we decided that it wouldn't be complete without Benedict's mother and Janet here. So we got on to the telephone on Friday and made all the arrangements.'

'And we were delighted to be invited.' Helen smiled at the young woman her son had married before her eyes moved to the tall figure standing just behind. 'And you couldn't have chosen a more glorious day for it. Now what were you doing, Victoria, when we came into the room?' she added. 'You seemed to be struggling with something that really could do with Benedict's help.'

Victoria felt a faint warmth in her cheeks, wishing that her weaknesses were less transparent than they appeared to be. 'Oh, I didn't want to disturb him . . .' The words sounded lamely in her ears. '. . . He was busy with other things.' Conscious of three pairs of feminine eyes looking fondly at her pink cheeks, she forced herself to look round at Benedict with a smile. 'But I must remember that I'm no longer a bachelor girl who has to cope with all these little jobs herself. Please,' she spoke with a mocking admission of weakness which brought an immediate spark of amusement into his eyes, 'would you lift that bookcase so I can straighten the edge of the carpet?'

A moment later the small task was accomplished and Victoria, in response to her mother's request, was going across to the kitchen to ask Mrs Paige to take some tea into the sitting-room for the visitors.

'Victoria.' Her husband's peremptory tone halted her and she turned to see him close the door firmly and come across the tiled floor towards her.

'Yes?' Her tone was the belligerent one she had been using as a defence all day.

He was silent for a moment while his eyes raked her with the cold dislike she knew so well. 'You'll have to do better than that, you know. We had an agreement that we'd make these few days happy ones. I've tried to keep my part of the bargain.'

'Oh yes, you've done very well.' She made no attempt to hide the sarcasm in her voice. 'You really deserve an Oscar.' There was a betraying tremble in her voice and she felt her eyes sting.

'Maybe I don't have to try so hard as you apparently do.' A tiny sigh escaped his lips and there was a slight softening in his glacial manner. 'Acting, I mean.' Victoria knew that his sharp glance had noticed the way she had caught her lower lip between her teeth, that he saw the glitter of tears. 'But I know that it's a bit of a strain on you, Victoria. Anyway, you go on upstairs now,' abruptly he turned away from her, 'while I go and organise the tea. I'll meet you here in ten minutes and we'll try to make certain that the last act is something to remember.'

Victoria stood in the hallway without moving, watching him go over to the kitchen door and inside without looking round at her. She felt a sob welling up inside her, but stifled it quickly when she heard a footstep on the stairs behind her and turned to look into her father's indulgent, affectionate face.

'Just been up with the cases, Victoria. Benedict's mother is in the room above the garage and Janet in the small one next door—or vice-versa.' He grinned. 'I forget which case was which, but I don't suppose it matters. Were you pleased with the surprise, love?'

'Surprise?' She looked at him blankly, scarcely understanding what he had been saying, conscious only of the terrible aching pain in her chest. From behind the kitchen door she could hear the murmur of laughter where doubtless Benedict was continuing his act of being charming. If only they knew him as he really was, she thought hopelessly.

'Go on upstairs, Vicky.' There was tender understanding in her father's voice that threatened her hard-won self-control, and his reversion to the childish name made her long to learn her head against his chest and blurt out the whole complicated story. 'You look as if you could do with a rest—too much excitement for you all at once. I'll make an excuse for you.'

With an effort she pulled herself together and actually managed to smile up into her father's concerned face. 'I'm all right, Dad. As you say, just a bit tired, but I'll be fine when I've done my face and my hair. I won't be a minute.' Then before she could put herself too much to the test she whirled away from him and ran to the stairs. 'Tell them to pour out a cup of tea for me. I'll be with you all in just a minute.'

But before she reached her bedroom the smile had faded from her lips and the ache was back in her chest with renewed pressure. She leaned wearily against the closed door, closed her eyes for just a minute, then walked over to the dressing-table. To her surprise, none of the anguish she was experiencing showed on her face. Her cheek was just as smooth and the faintly flushed look suited her. Her hair was tumbled about her face, but a quick run through with a comb tidied it and a smear of lipstick made her feel much better, quite able to face whatever awaited her downstairs. She turned abruptly away from her own reflection and as she did so her eyes could scarcely avoid looking at the bed which dominated the room.

Had she really shared it with Benedict last night? It was hard to believe that you could lie so close to a man for all those hours without experiencing some deepened quality in their relationship. She had lain beside him through the night, not daring to relax her own calm even breathing until she was absolutely certain that he was asleep. And then she had stared into the blackness of the night for all the endless hours that lay before the dawn.

But quite suddenly she was being wakened by the sound of curtains being pulled back and by the brilliance of the morning sunshine spilling across the room.

'I brought you some tea.'

Victoria put up a hand to push back the heavy swathe of hair that fell over her face and looked up into Benedict's enigmatic features. He was

casually dressed, suitably for the work that lay
ahead of all of them that day, with the sleeves of
his pale grey shirt rolled back over his muscular
forearms. She wrenched her eyes away from his
and struggled into a sitting position, immediately
regretting it when she sensed his gaze lingering over
her bare shoulders.

'Thank you.' One hand she put out to take the
cup from him, the other she used to clutch the sheet
higher about her.

'Oh, it was your mother's idea.' His eyes were
frankly derisive now as he stood looking down
at her, leaning with one hand against the wardrobe.
'Think nothing of it. I was only too pleased to
have the excuse to come up and *see* my wife in
bed.'

Victoria tried to sip her tea, giving no indication
of how his presence was affecting her. 'What time
is it?' She forgot about the clock by the bedside
until she had asked the question.

'The time is . . .' he shot a lazy glance at the gold
watch on his wrist before returning his mocking
gaze to her face, '. . . almost nine o'clock. I tried to
persuade your mother that you might like to lie a
little longer.' He left his relaxed position by the
wardrobe and sauntered across to the bed, sitting
down so unexpectedly that Victoria withdrew her
feet as if she had been stung. 'I told her that you
hadn't slept much and . . .'

'Why should you say any such thing?' The only
defence she had was to make her voice as cool and
uninvolved as she could. 'I slept perfectly well!' She
tried to ignore the questioning lift of one eyebrow.
'I ought to have been up ages ago.' She hoped he

wouldn't notice the way her heart was hammering against her ribs and she drew the sheet a little higher.

'Did you, Victoria?' His smile was disbelieving. 'Well . . .' he put out a hand for the empty cup, allowing his fingers to rest accidentally against hers for a moment, '. . . perhaps I was wrong. Anyway, your mother's eyes were mistily romantic when I told her, so perhaps the lie doesn't matter too much.' And before Victoria could think of a suitably smart reply the door of the bedroom was closing behind him.

She knew that he had been quite deliberately baiting her, but never in her life had she felt less like being amused. And that feeling of almost cataclysmic depression had lasted throughout the day, drowning every other sensation she was likely to have. Even now, when she had no choice but to go downstairs and join her parents with Helen and Janet in the sitting-room, she had to make a conscious effort so that she would be able to face Benedict. Victoria turned again towards the mirror, watching closely while she tried to curve her lips into a facsimile of the smile that would be expected from a newly-married girl. Then resolutely she turned again to go downstairs.

And by the time she was ready for the party in the evening, her determination was beginning to have some effect. Besides, it was impossible to remain depressed for long with such a stir of activity and celebration about her. Through the wide open windows of the bedroom she could even hear the sound of microphones being tested, evidence that

the disco which was to play for the dancing later
was in safe hands.

The guests were due to arrive at seven, and it
was fifteen minutes before that when Victoria
turned round in response to a knock at her door.
Her heart was hammering as she turned to face
Benedict when he came inside. He was dressed as
he had been when she saw him last, in a dark dinner
jacket, and he stood for a moment leaning back
against the door, looking, then he walked slowly
towards her. One hand was behind his back, the
other slipped into the pocket of his jacket. He
stopped, regarding her gravely, then as if recognis-
ing her anxiety, his lips curved into a smile.

'You look quite . . . beautiful, Victoria.' There
was no mockery about him now.

'Oh . . .' Unable to bear the sudden explosion of
pleasure his approval had brought, she turned
round to the mirror again, her hands reaching up
to touch the curls that had escaped from her swept-
back hairstyle. 'Oh, thank you.' She laughed, a low
satisfied sound. 'You don't think the dress is a bit
too . . .'

'Turn round.' His voice was sensuous, throbbing.
'So I can see you properly.' But his eyes holding
hers in the glass seemed to have a hypnotic quality,
denying her the power of movement. She saw him
step closer, saw the hand come from his pocket,
touch the bare skin of her shoulder. She shivered a
little as his fingers scorched her flesh, then responding to his insistence she turned round to face
him.

'No.' With apparent reluctance his eyes left her
face, took in the lines of the elegant dress, the halter

neckline suspended on a single cord which tied at the back of her neck, leaving her shoulders and back bare, the soft folds of cream material which fell to the ground with graceful simplicity. 'The dress is quite perfect, Victoria. You must know that.' His eyes were back on her face, moving with that faintly menacing assurance from her lips to her throat and back to her eyes.

'There's this jacket to go with it.' Breathing rather rapidly through slightly parted pink lips, Victoria reached out a nerveless hand towards the tiny bolero which was lying on the dressing-stool. 'Do you think I should put it on?'

The silence seemed to stretch on and on while his eyes continued to burn into hers. 'Perhaps . . .' at last he replied, 'perhaps with the jacket it would be more of a bride's dress.'

'Oh . . .' For no reason that she could explain his words had hurt and Victoria looked down as she struggled to find the sleeves, then recoiled as his hand came out to help her, lightly brushing her unprotected skin. 'Is that better?' She faced him defiantly.

'Better?' She caught a flicker of amusement in his eyes. 'I told you the dress was perfect before, so how could it be better now?' But suddenly he seemed to weary of the discussion about her dress and from behind his back he produced a cluster of tiny rosebuds. 'I thought these would be the right colour for you to wear.'

'Oh . . .' She put out a hand to touch the glossy dark green leaves and the creamy perfect blossoms. 'Oh, they're gorgeous, Benedict!'

'And I've even got one for myself.' He turned to

the mirror, slipping a matching rose into his buttonhole. His keen eyes were missing nothing of her
reaction to his unexpected little gesture. 'Your
mother suggested that you would prefer a spray to
wear at the back of your head, so . . .'

'Oh.' Once again she was unreasonably dashed
by his words. But what difference did it make if it
had been entirely her mother's idea? Resolutely she
thrust the question from her mind and turned
round to him with a happy expression. 'Will you
fix them on for me, Benedict?' Waiting for his
answer, she held her breath.

'Of course.' He seemed to find nothing strange
in the request and she watched in the glass as he
frowned over the complexity of the task she had
given him. 'But you mustn't expect too much. I'm
not an expert in these matters, you know.'

'You surprise me,' she replied demurely, wondering why she was feeling so unexpectedly lighthearted.

'Do I?' Suddenly looking up, he caught her mischievous expression, but instead of the response she
had hoped for there was a change in his expression,
the tawny eyes were dark and menacing as a jungle
animal's. 'Do I, Victoria?' His hands were hard
now on her shoulders, savagely turning her round
to face him. 'Do I?' he asked again, then his face
came towards hers, his mouth demanding and forceful closed on hers while his hands slipped down
her body, scorching through the sheer material of
her dress as if it had simply melted away.

For a moment only she was able to resist him,
before the clamouring demands of her own longing
weakened any resolve she might have thought she

had. Then with a submissive little sigh she allowed her lips to be parted, rejoicing in the swift upsurge of desire that quickened her pulse with an insistent throb. Tenderly now his mouth explored hers, then expertly, sensuously moved to her throat and on to the swell of her breast, warm and vulnerable beneath the sheer silk of her dress.

'Victoria.' His voice was deep and husky when at last he pulled himself away, looking down with a disturbed, indecipherable expression into her soft bewildered eyes. 'Victoria, I . . .' But before she could hear what he wanted to say someone knocked at the door, apologetic but insistent.

'Are you nearly ready, darlings?' It was Mrs Kendall's voice. 'A car is just turning into the drive, so I think . . .'

'It's all right, Mother.' Victoria was the first to find her voice. 'Benedict and I are just coming.' And she put her hand round to touch the spray of flowers at the back of her head, refusing now to look at him. 'Thank you.' Her voice was cold, a complete denial of the disturbed, passionate emotion that had surged through her a moment earlier but which was now receding leaving her drained. She turned abruptly aside, then when his hand came out towards her she made a show of drawing away from him with a tiny gesture of distaste.

'Victoria . . .' The word was almost stifled on his lips as he saw her antagonism and his hand dropped to his side.

'We'd better go. They'll be waiting for us.'

'Does that matter so much?' Now his manner matched hers for coldness.

'Of course it does.' Deliberately she tried to be flippant. 'As you said, we owe it to them all . . .'

'But there are other things we owe to each other.' He went over, holding the door while she walked through, and she could not resist looking into his cold eyes.

They stood together by the door of the marquee welcoming the guests as they arrived, and it was strange to reflect that they gave the appearance of a perfect couple while emotionally they were light years apart. Victoria felt that the curve of her lips had become a frozen travesty as she introduced all her friends to the tall familiar figure whom she had married. And Benedict, equally, played his role to perfection. No one watching would have suspected that his protective manner was sheer pretence, that the loving, smiling face he turned towards his bride was simple a façade.

Nor that in place of a heart she had a solid block of ice. Automatically she held out her hand, responded to the familiar jokes, laughed, made excuses, accepted the compliments with grace, all in spite of the terrible pain, the agonising resentment she was nurturing against the man at her side.

How dared he? That was the only thing in her mind at that time. How dared he continually take advantage of her weakness? How dared he imagine that simply because she had married him . . . But how dare you, Victoria?, a voice deep inside her was asking. How dare you be so cold and resentful, how dare you spurn your natural inclinations? Would it not be better, the same treacherous voice was asking, to settle for what you can get? Why cry for the moon? And why not use him as he has used you?

'Victoria!' She found both her hands clasped with such fervour that she was brought back to the present to find that she had just welcomed Mr and Mrs Westmacott and that now Iain was smiling down at her with every sign of besotted admiration. 'You're looking perfectly marvellous, my sweet!' And irresistibly she was pulled against him, while he kissed her cheek.

'Oh, Iain!' For a moment she had the urge to cling to him, to lie safely, unexcitingly on his chest until all her pain was soothed away. 'Iain,' a faint sob rose to her lips although they continued to smile, 'how wonderful to see you!' Almost at once she regained control of herself, withdrawing from the circle of his arms in spite of their reluctance to release her. Conscious of the impassive expression on Benedict's face as she introduced the two men, she could see that in other circumstances a storm would have been brewing.

'I'm glad to meet you at last.' If Iain was aware of any tension he gave no sign. 'I was sorry to miss you that day in London.'

'Yes.' In spite of the affectionate look he cast in her direction, Benedict left Victoria in no doubt about his feelings. 'I had another engagement that day. But I'm glad Victoria was able to keep you company.'

'Oh, she did that all right.' Iain's eyes lingered admiringly on her flushed cheeks. 'In fact I'm hoping that when I go down next I'll be able to persuade her to repeat the formula.'

'Next time,' Benedict interrupted smoothly linking possessive fingers about her wrist, 'I hope she'll invite you to the house. You know she's a super cook and she'll enjoy showing off to you.'

'That I can endorse.' Iain spoke with his usual amiable acquiescence. 'When I used to visit her at the flat I always told her she was wasting her talents with shorthand and typing.' And without waiting to see the response to his compliment he went forward to speak to Helen, who was standing on Benedict's right.

Victoria was grateful that her mother chose that moment to desert her position by the opening of the marquee and suggest that as all the guests seemed to have arrived, perhaps it was time for them to relax a bit, to begin to enjoy themselves. 'Besides,' she continued, 'we're the only ones who haven't had any champagne yet and I'm sure Benedict's longing for something to drink. Now, where did Janet go to?'

And it was a relief for Victoria to have the excuse to break away from the intimate little group by the door and begin to speak to the visitors in a less formal situation. The hours seemed simply to fly past and at last the remains of the buffet meal were cleared away and the guests were relaxing round the small tables sipping coffee, talking and laughing while moths fluttered, bewildered, round the softly illuminated pink lamps.

Victoria was leaning against one of the supports, enjoying the cool evening air on her warm cheeks when fingers took the empty glass she was cradling in her hands. 'Have you had something to eat, Victoria?' She turned round to look into Benedict's impassive face then, unable to bear it, quickly looked away again.

'I did have something.' She tried to concentrate on what she was saying. 'But I put my plate down to speak to someone and when I looked again it had been taken away.'

'And champagne? How many glasses have you had?'

'Just one,' she said mournfully. 'Only someone kept refilling it.'

'Victoria!' There was amused reproof in his voice. 'Come on, then.' He put an irresistible hand under her elbow and led her out of the marquee round to a little seat under the shelter of a climbing rose. 'I refuse to have the first waltz with a girl who's unsteady on her feet. I've got some food for you here.' And he produced a plate with some slices of smoked duck and tongue, tomato and pepper salad and a roll spread with butter. 'Now,' he shook out a large white napkin and pushing her gently on to the seat spread it out on her knee, 'eat this while I go and find some black coffee for both of us.'

By the time he returned carrying a tray with cups and a pot of coffee Victoria had almost demolished the food and a moment later wiped her mouth with a sigh of satisfaction. 'Thank you.' A faint smile touched her lips. 'I wondered why I was feeling so lightheaded.' She put out a hand to take the cup he was offering her and sipped the strong dark brew gratefully. 'I hadn't realised ... All that champagne on an empty stomach.'

'I should hate, Victoria ...' there was a vague regret in his voice that brought panic hammering into her throat again, '. . . I should hate all these upright citizens of Harrogate to think I'd driven you to the bottle already.'

This time the sob that had been aching in her chest for so long would not be controlled. 'You haven't.' Tears stung at her eyes. 'Oh, you haven't!'

At that very moment the music, which had been soft and subdued all evening, was interrupted by the voice of the disc jockey, loud and intrusive over the address system, and its very power meant that for a little while Victoria was unable to understand what was being said.

'I think they're waiting for us.'

She stared into his eyes, searching in the darkness in an attempt to discern his expression. And then she heard her own name. And his.

'The bride and bridegroom,' the unseen voice insisted. 'Could we have Victoria and Benedict to begin the evening's dancing?'

'Oh, must we?'

There was an instant's silence and she thought she saw a flash of anger from his eyes just then. 'I'm afraid we must, my sweet.' Surely his voice had hardened just a shade? 'Tonight we must do what's expected of us. As you so forcibly reminded me earlier this evening, we owe it to them.'

CHAPTER TEN

By two o'clock most of the older guests including Mr and Mrs Kendall, Helen and Janet had left, only the young ones, Victoria's own friends, remaining to swirl and gyrate to the subdued throb of the music.

'I hope your parents will be able to get to sleep with all the din, Victoria.'

'What?' She looked up into Iain's face, at the same time trying to ease herself out of the tight embrace in which he held her.

'Your parents.' He smiled, looking she thought faintly foolish with his usually immaculate blond hair slightly dishevelled and his tie askew.

'Oh,' said Victoria, still not understanding what he meant. She was more interested in watching Benedict and the way he was looking down at Jane Ellerbeck. Now Jane was just his type, she decided bleakly. She was tall and lean to the point of emaciation, had just got rid of one husband and was very obviously on the lookout for someone to replace him.

'Not that that means marriage,' she had confided to Victoria when they had gone upstairs to repair their make-up an hour earlier. 'I've had enough of that for the time being thank you very much. Pity,' carefully she outlined the full pouting lips with red, 'pity I'm too late to give you a warning, but,' she pressed her lips together and surveyed herself with

174

satisfaction in the mirror, 'you were probably too besotted to pay any attention. Not that I blame you, mind. A man like Benedict must be pretty hard to resist. I expect he's a fabulous lover.' She ran a comb through her long blonde hair without seeming to notice the effect her words were having on her friend. 'Men like that always are—so much experience, I suppose. That's what was wrong with Jack and me. He had none when we got married, but seemed to think it was his duty to get as much as he could *after* that. And of course he resented me having the same idea. But you're lucky, Victoria.' She sighed, suddenly mournful. 'I think I'll come to London. Men like Benedict just·don't seem to exist this far north.'

And the way Benedict was looking at his partner and laughing made Victoria wonder if perhaps the admiration Jane had shown was being reciprocated.

'Iain,' suddenly she linked her hands about his neck, 'I would like a breath of air—I'm so warm with dancing.'

'Warm?' He looked down at her in disbelief and pleasure. 'In that dress?' His eyes lingered over her shoulders, bare now that her jacket was lying discarded on one of the chairs. 'But nothing, my sweet, would give me greater pleasure.' His hands about her waist slipped lower as he guided her round the floor in the direction of the wide flaps of the marquee.

It was only when they reached the end of the garden that it occurred to Victoria that perhaps Iain too had had a little too much to drink. Certainly his arm about her shoulders was a bit persistent and no matter how much she moved away from him he refused to allow her to escape. And when they reached the end of the path and she tried to turn back his bulk blocked her way.

'Victoria.' The smell of liquor was on his breath as his face loomed close to hers and she could hear his hurried excited breathing. 'Victoria.' Strong fingers bit into her shoulders, pulling her tightly to him, his mouth was against her neck, wet and somehow, disgusting.

'Iain.' Her heart was hammering, but from fear this time, and she was wondering if she would be heard if she cried out.

'This is what you wanted, isn't it?' His chin nuzzled roughly against her cheek. 'Asking me to come out here with you.'

'Of course it wasn't.' With an immense effort she thrust his face away from her and laughed, determined to keep some kind of control of the situation. 'I simply felt warm and asked you to bring me out for a breath of air.'

'You can't fool me, Victoria,' he laughed unpleasantly. 'You and Benedict have fallen out, that's what it is. And you want to score against him. Well, I don't mind being part of your plan. You know I've always wanted you, Victoria, right from the beginning I fancied you. Even more now you're married—experienced!' he laughed.

'Don't be silly, Iain.' Now she tried to be brisk and matter-of-fact, although it wasn't easy when she was trying to escape from his searching mouth. 'You're going to feel an idiot in the morning. And so am I next time we meet. Iain, please ....'

'Do as my wife asks, Westmacott.' The icy tones

that cut through the softness of the warm air brought Iain's head up with a jerk and the involuntary slackening of his arms enabled Victoria to twist out of his reach. Shivering suddenly, she leaned against the stone upright of the rose pergola, quite unable to turn in the direction of the tall shadowy figure who stood just within her field of vision. From the corner of her eye she could see the glowing end of a cigar move upwards to his mouth and down again. Iain was in front of her and she saw him, still breathing noisily, look from her to Benedict and back again, obviously unable to think of anything to say. At last Benedict stepped towards them and spoke again. Only someone knowing him as well as Victoria did would have had any idea that he was ferociously but icily angry. The mildness of manner was something she had learned over the years to dread.

'Thank you for looking after Victoria, but now I'm able to take over myself. Oh, and by the way, I've told Jane Ellerbeck that you might give her a lift home. She's ready to go now.'

'Oh ... Oh ... all right.' Iain raked his hand through his hair in a bewildered way and turning, walked fairly steadily back along the path to the house.

Victoria stood watching him until she saw him turn round into the pool of light that spilled from the marquee and disappear. Still she refused to turn to Benedict, although she knew that he was looking at her with the searching intense gaze that always preceded a kill.

'Your guests are waiting to say goodbye to you.' Like an automaton she moved away from the supporting pillar and along the path in the direction of the marquee, until the vehemence of his expletive brought her whirling round to face him.

'Damn you, Victoria!' The harsh anger of his voice made her eyes widen in sudden terror and she put up a hand as if to ward off a blow.

'Yes,' there was a cold laughing sneer on his lips as at last she forced herself to look at him, 'we have something to learn from the caveman who used to beat his wife into submission. If she misbehaved in front of guests there was one quick sure way of bringing her back under his control. In fact . . .' he laughed again, this time with a more menacing, faintly amused sound, 'in fact, my dear wife, you've given me an idea.' And before she was aware of what he was doing she felt herself swept up into his arms and they were striding along the path towards the marquee.

There was a gasp as they entered and the few couples who were still there stared for a moment, then one or two began to laugh and clap. 'Well done, Benedict!' Josh Allbright, who had known Victoria since they had started kindergarten together, grinned down into her flushed face and gently pulled a strand of her hair. 'There's been too much of this Women's Lib. It's time some of the men struck back!'

Benedict grinned as if it was all a great joke. 'Yes, we should try to revive some of those good old customs. Now I'm not actually asking you to come up to see that the bride's properly bedded, but . . .' He paused significantly.

'Oh, we get the idea.' Jane smiled down at Victoria before turning an admiring eye on

Benedict. 'What did I tell you, my sweet?' She bent and swiftly brushed her lips against Victoria's cheek. 'Anyway, Iain will be waiting at the front door. I've promised to drive the car home for him. Perhaps I might be able to persuade him to stay the night at my place!' And with a conspiratorial little grin at Victoria she walked away.

A few moments later, Benedict was elbowing his way into the house and across the hall towards the stairs. Victoria struggled for a moment, then finding the only effect of that was to increase the pressure from his arms she resorted to verbal attack.

'Would you please put me down!' she snapped through clenched teeth. 'You've caused a big enough sensation to satisfy even your thirst for publicity. You can't do any more, as there's no one to see.'

'Oh yes, I can.' His reply was equally terse and tight-lipped. 'I can do what I should have done weeks ago.'

Victoria felt her heart begin to hammer at first softly, then with increasing agitation against her chest. 'What . . . what do you mean?'

'I mean,' he sneered softly, 'exactly what you think I mean.'

'If you do . . .' Much of the fierce self-assurance had fled from her voice as he climbed the stairs. 'If you do, then I shall scream and everyone will hear—your mother, Janet, my mother and . . .'

'Your parents are old enough to know that girls, especially newly married ones, sometimes call out in pleasure.' They reached the door of their bedroom and without releasing his hold on her, Benedict turned the knob then pushed the door closed by leaning against it.

'Men!' She spat the word with all the venom that the stillness of the house permitted. 'Always you think of only one thing!'

He laughed softly, at the same time allowing her to slide from his arms so that her feet touched the floor while still anchoring her very definitely against him with his hands pressing on her hips. 'I can't deny, my sweet, that at this minute my mind is very definitely on one thing. In fact,' in the softly lighted rooms all signs of amusement faded from his expression, 'more and more I begin to wonder what possessed me to think . . .' Abruptly he stopped, but not before Victoria had understood exactly what he had meant.

In an instant all the throbbing intensity of her body was replaced by a cold stillness. Even the anger she had felt for him was gone and at the same time she felt his arms slacken so that she was able to step away from him and go towards the dressing table. She sank down on to the stool, looking at her own reflection, but seeing only his figure leaning against the door. Methodically she put up her hands to remove the dangling gold earrings which had pleased her so much earlier. She placed them on the small crystal tray, then pulled from her left hand the glittering stone which had been hers for so short a time.

'Yes, Benedict.' She spoke with the calmness of despair and with the softness that showed her subconscious awareness of her parents sleeping a short distance away. 'That's a question most people would find difficult to answer. What was it that made you think . . . I could see the same question in the eyes of everyone who was here tonight. What made you think that you'd ever be content with a wife like me?'

There was a long silence before she raised her eyes to look at him in the glass. As their eyes met, he took a step in her direction, shrugged and then smiled faintly, as if he were amused at himself.

'Curiously enough that wasn't what I meant. I can't even believe you want me to take what you've said seriously. You have only to look in the mirror, my sweet, and you'll find the answer. Why I . . .' the smile disappeared, 'and why Iain was only too willing . . .'

'Iain had had too much to drink, that's all.' Recollection brought fresh colour to her cheeks and she bit her lip.

'And you didn't encourage him. Not just a little?'

'Were you encouraging, as you put it, Jane Ellerbeck?' Victoria flashed back. 'Weren't you just loving it while she looked up at you all goofy-eyed?'

'Victoria!' There was a shade of menace back in his voice now. 'You almost sound as if you're jealous. If I thought that . . .'

'Of course I'm jealous!' Suddenly there seemed no point in dissembling any longer, in fact there was a positive masochistic pleasure in throwing at him all the misery he had caused her. What did it matter if his response was amusement and contempt? Would she be any worse off than she was now? She swung round in her seat to face him, so tall and calm, watching her closely with a curious expression on his face. 'Of course I'm jealous—

wildly jealous. Madly!' She tossed her head and told herself that it didn't matter if her parents were wakened by the row. 'Do you really think I don't care about your affairs with women? With the Baroness?' She rose and paced across the room, caring nothing that he should see her distracted expression. 'And with Jane.' The words spoken, the enormity of her own misery overwhelmed her and the tears began to streak down her cheeks, she no longer tried to control the sobs which shook her body.

'Hush, Victoria.' His arms came round her again, but this time gently, and she felt one hand hold her close while the other stroked the head that drooped against his chest. 'Hush, my darling—my sweet.' Incredibly she felt his mouth against her hair and her astonishment was so great that her tears, a moment earlier welling from an unfathomable source, suddenly dried up.

'Benedict?' Queryingly she raised her face to his, felt the comfort of a large white handkerchief wiping the dampness from her face. 'Benedict?' she repeated, disturbed by the expression she imagined she could read in his eyes.

'First of all, my darling,' and his tongue lingered over the endearment quite as if he meant it, 'I never had an affair with Camilla and . . .'

'Never?' In spite of herself Victoria could not conceal the incredulity his denial caused.

He shook his head and smiled. 'Never. And as to your friend Jane, I was trying to be interested in her for your sake. While all the time I was longing to be dancing with my wife.'

Search as she might for some indication that he

was joking, she could see none. In spite of the anguish of past experience she felt a flicker of emotion begin to stir at the base of her spine—a flicker that was fanned into a flame when his hands slid down, imprisoning her firmly against his long taut body. 'With . . . me?' She spoke faintly, her eyes watching the curve of his mouth.

'With you, my darling.' His hands pressed her even more possessively against him.

'But you said a moment ago . . .' Disturbingly his mouth came down to brush against hers, making her forget what she was about to say.

'A moment ago, I said . . .' The words were whispered against her cheek as his lips caressed her cheek.

'You said . . .' she was almost too breathless to speak, but she raised her head joyfully as Benedict's mouth pressed against the hollow of her throat, 'you didn't know what had possessed you to think that you . . .' She broke off with a faint moan while her mind was desperately trying to remember exactly what he had said.

'I don't know what possessed me to think that if we married we would lead placid lives with none of the turmoil that intense involvement brings. No sooner do I find myself married to the calm cool Miss Kendall than I find her transformed into the intense, sensuous Mrs Benedict Gabriell. Whom I daren't touch in case she guesses the tumult she's causing in my normally ordered life. See here.' He took her hand and slipped it inside his jacket where she could feel the rapid powerful beating of his heart. 'And I can feel yours.' Looking down at her, he put his hand on the curve of her breast with such tenderness that she felt a whole maelstrom of emotions melt and conjoin within her.

'I love you, Victoria. I adore you. The only thing I regret is . . .' The words faded as he pressed his cheek against hers again and his arms began to hold her more closely, more forcefully to the demanding strength of his body.

'Your only regret . . .' The words escaped from breathless lips that turned searchingly towards his, rejoicing in the faint roughness, abrasive on her soft flesh.

'My only regret is that I didn't set myself out to court you, to woo you properly, to sweep you off your feet. Now, if it's not too late, I want to do that.'

Touched by the diffidence which she had never heard in his voice before, Victoria whispered, 'It's not too late.' Then with a tiny laugh almost stifled as she brushed his mouth with her lips, 'For a rather intelligent man, Benedict Gabriell, I think you've been pretty slow on the uptake!'

'Tell me.' The words were confident, masterful, the manner dominating as he caught her hair in one hand and held her away from him. 'Tell me, Victoria.' But the smile at his mouth, the gleam of passion in the tawny eyes spoke of more subtle, complex emotions.

'I love you.' It was the most natural thing in the world to link her hands about his neck, urging him again towards her. 'I love you,' she repeated seriously.

'When?' he insisted. 'When did you first realise?'

The smile that curved her mouth now was very sure. 'Since almost that first day in your office.

You were right, you see . . .'

'How crazy I must have been! Not to see what was absolutely under my nose. But what do you mean, I was right?'

'To be wary of any young girl who came to work for you. I was bound to fall in love with you. Otherwise,' she teased, 'I doubt if I would have stayed.'

'Am I such a bad employer?' Benedict relaxed his grip on her hair and brought her head back to rest on his shoulder.

'Awful,' she said happily, dreamily. 'So much so that I used to think if you had a wife I'd pity her.'

'And do you?' he murmured into her hair.

'Now,' she shook her head, 'now I think that to be your wife is exactly my idea of heaven.'

'If I can make it that for you,' his voice was deep and husky and he forced up her head with his chin in urgent longing for her mouth, 'then assuredly it will be that for both of us. Your mother was right, my darling. *This* was our wedding day, that other just a date on the calendar.' Then his fingers were impatiently pulling at the string at the back of her neck and he was carrying her across to the inviting softness of the large bed.

Victoria lay watching the first pink streaks of dawn appear in the sky to the east, a smile touched her lips as she remembered the previous night and how they had slept with a pillow down the middle of the bed. But now they were truly one flesh. That was what it meant. Dreamily, with a sense of wonder, she allowed her hand to drift down over her breast, recalling with a faint indrawn gasp the indescribable pleasure of Benedict's expert, tender lovemaking. Then her fingers, moving over her satisfied body encountered, were at once enclosed by his. She heard him murmur her name as he pulled her possessively, sensuously against him, turning her so that they lay facing each other, their heads very close on the pillows.

'Can't you sleep?' In the almost dark the tawny eyes gleamed.

'I don't want to.' As she whispered she moved so that their lips like the whole length of their bodies just touched and she raised her hands to link them about his neck, her fingers stroking gently.

His laugh was low and deep and satisfied. 'Would your mother mind if we decided to spend the rest of the day in bed?'

'She'd think we were crazy!'

'I am crazy. And I can't tell you how much I'm enjoying the feeling.'

'Tell me,' Victoria's lips moved appealingly against his, 'tell me when you first realised,' she remembered the words he had used to her earlier, 'that life with me was going to be less placid than you'd meant it to be.'

'So that's what your devious little mind has been worrying about!' His fingers trickled down her spine. 'Are you sure you can't think of something better to do at the moment?'

'I can.' Her whisper was almost stifled by his mouth moving tantalisingly against hers. 'But first I want to know that.'

'Well,' he sighed in mock resignation, 'I first realised on our wedding afternoon when we were sitting having tea together. And then later, that evening when Jeremy Ransome came over with that dumb bird, I knew I wanted nothing so much as to be rid of them. And . . .'

'But I thought that you were just embarrassed that he talked about Camilla.'

'Camilla?' His laugh was a trifle rueful. 'Ah yes, Camilla. I suppose I treated her rather badly.'

'Were you in love with her?'

'No, of course not. Otherwise I might have married her. That was what she obviously wanted, what she was holding out for. Then I found out that she'd leaked the story of our impending marriage to one of the gossip columns. A friend of mine works on the paper and I soon knew that the tale had come direct from Camilla. I'm afraid it gave me a great deal of satisfaction to squash the rumour in the firmest way possible. I feel a bit ashamed, my darling, that I used you to do it.' His mouth brushed tantalisingly against hers. 'No, I don't. What am I saying? It was the wisest thing I ever did in my life. So sensible, in fact, that I think it must have been a subconscious idea just waiting to be recognised. Can you forgive me?'

'I'm trying to.' It was a low, mischievous whisper against his cheek. 'And I'm even beginning to feel a bit sorry for Camilla. That day when I found her in your bedroom with Lumsden . . .'

'Oh, Lumsden. You know that he's her cousin.'

'Her cousin!'

'Perhaps not exactly her cousin—second cousin possibly. In any case, it was she who asked me to take him on when the Jacksons retired. Anyway, I've quite decided that when we go back I'll ask him to find somewhere else. He'll have no problem getting another job and I would prefer you to stay at home. I can't tell you how distracting it's been with you in the office and me feeling as I do . . .' His lips brushed tantalisingly against hers. '. . . You'll never know just how close to danger you came. Especially that day when I overheard you speaking to Iain.'

'And all the time you were planning to lunch with Camilla!' she pouted reprovingly.

'Not just with her.' His hands slipped round her waist and tightened menacingly. 'Jeremy and two other chaps were supposed to be there, but dropped out. Besides, it was supposed to be a working lunch. You know that Camilla has some business interests in the company Daniel runs. Yes, and that meeting with him . . .'

'Oh, I know about that.' Victoria felt her cheeks colour guiltily. 'I found out later that he'd come back unexpectedly and that you'd met him at the airport, but I couldn't bring myself to admit that I was wrong. Miriam rang me the following day and I was able to pretend that I knew all about it . . . I was ashamed to let you know.'

Benedict's laugh was quiet but not without a note of triumph. 'I think it was that, my sweet, which first indicated that perhaps I had some grounds for hope. Was it possible you were jealous? Then I began to reflect on what Mother had said that day when we were in Cornwall and it occurred to me to wonder exactly why you'd decided to marry me. You see, although you made me furious at the time I couldn't accept your explanation. That's when I first began to plan a honeymoon, one that I thought might turn out to be a real honeymoon. Not one with me relegated to the garden shed or where our bed had a bolster lying down the middle like some implacable duenna.'

Victoria moved her hands lightly, tantalisingly over his chest, feeling the hair move springily beneath her fingers. 'There's nothing between us now.'

'No.' His voice was husky and he pushed her back against the pillows, supporting himself on one elbow as he looked down at her. 'No, there's nothing between us now, my darling.' His hands on her silky skin caused her breathing to quicken as the sensuous pulse of desire began to mount inside her. 'And on Monday, my sweet, we're going to fly off to Sri Lanka and all day we're going to lie on the beaches. And all night I'm going to make love to you.'

'No Berber tents? No churches of Moscow?' Her voice was drowsy as she pulled his head down to hers.

'Those, my darling, are for another time. This is the time for pleasure.' And together they drifted off to Paradise.

Best Seller Romances

Romances you have loved

Each month, Mills & Boon publish four Best Seller Romances. These are the love stories that have proved particularly popular with our readers — they really are 'back by popular demand'. All give you the chance to meet fascinating people. Many are set in exotic faraway places.

If you missed them first time around, or if you'd like them as presents for your friends, look out for Mills & Boon Best Sellers as they are published. And be sure of the very best stories in the world of romance.

On sale where you buy paperbacks. If you have any difficulty obtaining them write to: Mills & Boon Reader Service, P.O. Box 236, Thornton Rd, Croydon, Surrey CR9 3RU, England. Readers in South Africa — please write to Mills & Boon Reader Service of Southern Africa, Private Bag X3010, Randburg 2125, S. Africa.

Mills & Boon
the rose of romance

Fall in love with Mills & Boon

Do you remember the first time you fell in love? The heartache, the excitement, the happiness? Mills & Boon know – that's why they're the best-loved name in romantic fiction.

The world's finest romance authors bring to life the emotions, the conflicts and the joy of true love, and you can share them – between the covers of a Mills & Boon.

We are offering you the chance to enjoy ten specially selected Mills & Boon Romances absolutely FREE and without obligation. Take these free books and you will meet ten women who must face doubt, fear and disappointment before discovering lasting love and happiness.

--✄----------

To: Mills & Boon Reader Service,
   FREEPOST, PO Box 236, Croydon, Surrey CR9 9EL.

Please send me, free and without obligation, ten Mills & Boon Romances, and reserve a Reader Service Subscription for me. If I decide to subscribe I shall from the beginning of the month following my free parcel of books, receive 10 new books each month for £8.50, post and packing free. If I decide not to subscribe, I shall write to you within 21 days, but whatever I decide the free books are mine to keep. I understand that I may cancel my subscription at any time simply by writing to you. I am over 18 years of age.

Please write in BLOCK CAPITALS

Name_____

Address_____

_____

_____

_____ Post Code_____

Offer applies in the UK only. Overseas send for details.
SEND NO MONEY – TAKE NO RISKS   XR2